American Diaries

DISCARD

ROSA MORENO

HOLLYWOOD, CALIFORNIA, 1934

⟨⟩

by Kathleen Duey

D0067754

cop.1

⟨⟩

Aladdin Paperbacks

New York   London   Toronto   Sydney   Singapore

For Richard
For Ever

If you purchased this book without a cover you should be aware
that this book is stolen property. It was reported as "unsold and
destroyed" to the publisher and neither the author nor the publisher
has received any payment for this "stripped book."

First Aladdin Paperbacks edition November 1999

Copyright © 1999 by Kathleen Duey

Aladdin Paperbacks
An imprint of Simon & Schuster
Children's Publishing Division
1230 Avenue of the Americas
New York, NY 10020

All rights reserved, including the right of
reproduction in whole or in part in any form.

The text for this book was set in Fairfield.
Printed and bound in the United States of America
10 9 8 7 6 5 4 3 2 1

ISBN 0-689-83126-9

Sunday, June 25 by now, I bet. I am not going to go look at the kitchen clock to find out! Mrs. Carillo's roosters haven't started up yet, so it has to be before four or five o'clock.

I have been awake off and on all night. I don't have a new book to read so I was trying to write a story about a girl whose father buys her a horse, but I can't think straight enough to write anything. Oh, how these curlers hurt. My scalp aches, and Mama won't be up for hours. She is so sure leaving my hair rolled up twice as long will work. I don't think it will, even if Monique at the beauty parlor said it might. My hair is just not meant to be curly. If Mama is right, I will only get to have the curlers out long enough to wash my hair and start over to get ready for Monday morning. Oh, joy.

I am nervous about this audition. Worse than usual. Mama is convinced I am perfect for this part. It's a Jane Withers kind of role—lots of comedy, lots of personality, and not too Goody-Two-shoes. So maybe they will consider a dark-haired girl. Mama says I dance as well as or better than Shirley Temple ever will, and that it is time for there to be another brunette sweetheart in the spotlight. Baby Peggy had wonderful dark hair, she says. And I always want to say, "Yes, and it was straight as a stick, just like mine." But I know what she would answer. She would just arch her painted-on brows at me and put her hands on her hips and say, "That was before Miss Shirley Temple came to town!"

I wish it wasn't Sunday, so we could go to the library today. Miss Campbell always finds me the perfect book—and if I had something to read, I wouldn't get so nervous. The curlers are in so tight, I have a headache. Mama doesn't understand with her blond hair that curls all by itself. I got Papa's hair, thick and dark and straight as anything.

Papa was a fine actor, and he would have become a star, Mama says. I counted up last time we went and I have seen his movies ten times apiece. We watch the ads for the B-movie houses and we cross the city if we have to, to see them. We don't go see the one he didn't finish, though Mama says one day I will want to, even if she never does.

They changed the script and made it so his character gets shot and dies just before the second reel. They used Pancho as a stand-in to film the death scene. Mama says she thinks it was terrible for Pancho to do. I think Papa would have wanted him to.

Mama hates horses. I don't. I only hate that one big bay gelding for falling on Papa. I was only five when he died but I remember his face clear as anything. His accent made his voice sound like music to me. Every time we visit his grave I pretend I can hear him talking to me.

* * *

I went back to sleep, and now the sun is out and bright. I got up to use the bathroom, and there is not a single sound coming from Mama's room yet. These curlers are about to make me scream. But I know she'll have a fit if I take them out. I looked at the kitchen clock when I was up. It's 11:15 now—so she should be up before long.

I had a dream about Papa, a nice one about him walking with me and laughing. Pancho came by last week. They all still do, sometimes, but he comes most often. They are all caballeros de las peliculas—movie cowboys, just like Papa. Mama says it was their fault Papa died, but I know she is wrong. It was just a bad horse—Jefe and Pancho have both told me that—a nervous animal that the director had no business using for a trip-line scene. I wish the director hadn't made them do the third take. I wish Papa had been on his usual, calm horse. I wish his friends could have helped him free of the saddle. I wish all this, every day. I miss my father so much.

Mama didn't like Pancho—or Jefe or Ruperto— or any of them, long before Papa got killed. She would always frown when they came to the door asking for Papa with their big sombreros tucked beneath their arms. Pancho still takes flowers to Papa's grave if he is working at Paramount up by the cemetery. We find old bouquets when we go to visit sometimes.

I feel sick thinking about tomorrow. Mama is so hopeful. But I am eleven and a half now. I am getting taller. Shirley Temple started at three and she's only six now. Jackie Coogan made his first film when he was little, too. Baby Peggy was a toddler! So many of the early fairy stars were washed up before they were twelve. Mama says they didn't make it when talkies started, because they had bad, squeaky voices or couldn't manage clear elocution or something. But other people say it was because they just got less cute and less fun to watch. So why am I even bothering to try now?

I like extra work. I love the sets and watching how the lights are moved around and how they make things look different in the film from how they looked on the set. If I could just be an extra forever, I would be happy standing around watching the movies get made. It is so interesting

Maybe I will make it tomorrow, maybe some kind of magic will happen, and they will choose me. But I see the same girls at the auditions over and over, and many of them are prettier and some are better at dancing at five or six than I will ever be, whether Mama admits it or not.

Oh, she will be furious if she reads this. Sometimes I think she does. Sometimes I wish she would. Then she would know that all this scares me.

Mama says I don't work hard enough. But I have worked very hard the past two years. Mrs. Meglin's classes helped a lot, and being chosen for her Famous Kiddies group has been fun. And Miss Gavin has been a great teacher. I can dance as well as most now, and my stage fright is almost gone when Meglin's Kiddies perform at department stores. But being part of the chorus line is a lot different from being out in front, alone, pretending to be someone else!

Mama, if you ever read this, and if I ever am a star, just remember, I did it for you. And for Papa.

CHAPTER ONE

Rosa opened her eyes. Her diary was still open face-down, balanced on her stomach. She blinked slowly once, then twice, playing a game she had invented when she was little. If she didn't move an inch, not a fraction of an inch, then the day wasn't really starting. It wasn't really tomorrow yet, and whatever she was worried about wasn't about to happen.

Eyes moving didn't count—today wouldn't start until she moved some part of her body besides her eyes, so Rosa let herself look toward the window. It was really bright out. It was probably going to be hot.

Rosa tried, for the hundredth time, to remember when she had made up the game, but she couldn't. She had been playing it as long as she could remember. She blinked again. The window was rimmed with bright sunlight seeping through the tiny spaces between the shade and the wall.

It was a stupid game, really, and Rosa knew it. She wasn't little anymore. But she was used to it, and it made her feel better, anyway, like looking under the bed to make sure that there weren't any bogeymen or other imaginary creatures. She *knew* there weren't, of course, but she felt better after she looked.

"Rosa?"

It was her mother's voice, soft and tentative. Rosa closed her eyes instantly, before she even heard the sound of her doorknob turning. She slid her diary beneath her pillow, then composed her face with the ease of any actress. She made herself look like someone sleeping, her mouth slightly open, her eyelids perfectly relaxed.

"Rosa?"

The door made the tiny wooden hiccuping sound that meant Mama was pushing against it. There was a second sound, the rubbing of the door itself against the jamb as Mama nudged it open. Rosa knew without looking that her mother would open the door only an inch or two, then peer through the crack into her room.

Without moving the tiniest muscle, Rosa counted the seconds as they went past. One, chimpanzee, two chimpanzee, three chimpanzee . . .

Rosa almost smiled. Her friend Callie had taught her that. The word "chimpanzee" was the perfect length to count seconds—it took exactly a second to say it. When a director wanted a two-beat pause, the chimpanzee count was just long enough. This morning, fifteen full chimpanzee-seconds clicked past before Mama spoke again.

"Rosita?"

The nickname sounded wrong the way Mama said it, with her soft, Virginia accent instead of Papa's musical Mexican one. But it worked. Rosa had a harder time pretending not to hear the name her father had always called her.

"I'm awake," Rosa admitted, opening her eyes and turning on her side to face the door.

"Good," Mama said. "Just give me time to use ice beneath my eyes. Looks like you could use some, too. We don't want any bumps and bags, do we?"

Rosa sat up very slowly. "The curlers hurt bad, Mama."

Mama opened the door the rest of the way and came in. Her hair needed fixing, too, Rosa saw. But Rosa was always proud of the way Mama looked when they went places. All the other mothers would look as perfect as they could, but Mama was always the prettiest one in any crowd. Rosa looked at her mother's curly blond hair and light blue eyes. If she could look like a five-year-old version of that—instead of an eleven-and-a-half-year-old version of herself, she might have already caught some director's eye. Most of the dark-haired girls played the nemesis parts, she knew; they were cast as bullies and gossips—or, like

Jane Withers, as spunky bad girls the audience loved for being naughty.

"Up, up," Mama was saying. She crossed the room and pulled up the shade. Rosa blinked.

"Come on, sweeties," Mama said quietly.

Rosa swung her feet to the floor, staring at her toes. They were already a little crooked. Not from her tap shoes, but from her pointe shoes—even though she was practicing ballet much less lately. Tap was all the rage now . . . in the movies and in the studios.

In every movie, almost, Shirley tapped her way through two or three numbers, singing in her clear, brassy little voice. Because of her, there were dance studios all across the country teaching girls to tap dance.

"You wash your face, I'll get ice," Mama said.

Rosa nodded and stood up, yawning, pulling her robe off the back of her chair. It was too big. Her mother had found it balled up beneath the makeup table of an MGM Studios dressing room. Someone had left it by mistake. Mama had shaken it out, humming, and laid it across the back of the chair. Four days later, when Rosa's scenes were all shot, it was still there. Mama had thrown it over her arm and they had walked out, just like that.

The robe had smelled of perfume at first, but finally, Rosa had had to wash it in the sink. Now it smelled like the cold cream Mama made her put on her face every night to keep her skin plump and smooth.

Rosa padded toward the bathroom at the end of the hall, holding the robe closed. She would always wonder which of the stars had left it lying where Mama had found it. It was silk, and except for a few makeup stains around the collar, there wasn't a thing wrong with it.

Rosa used the commode, then pulled the chain to flush it. Then, standing in front of the little mirror hung over the sink, she stared at herself. She was pretty; sort of, anyway. Her skin was darker than most of the other girls' who came to audition, but Mama kept saying that was good, that it made her stand out.

"Maybe," Rosa whispered to herself. She frowned back at herself in the mirror. "And maybe not."

"Here." Mama pushed open the bathroom door an inch or two, then peered inside, just as she had the bedroom door. Rosa reached out and pulled it open wide. She took the little muslin bag of shattered ice and held it over her left eye for a few seconds, then switched it to her right.

"Let's see," Mama said, coming close. Rosa could smell the coffee on her breath. She had been up awhile.

"Not too bad this morning," Mama said, running her thumb in a gentle curve beneath Rosa's eyes. "But let's use the ice again, just to be sure. You never know. We could end up running into some big director."

Rosa nodded. It almost never happened, but once in a while, some lucky boy or girl was discovered in a drugstore, or some other unlikely place. It made sense to always look her best. The little bags of ice, smashed to powder with the butt end of the ice pick, were a trick Mama's own mother had taught her.

Rosa felt a familiar ache. She had never met any of her grandparents. Mama's family had been furious when Mama had moved to Hollywood to become an actress, then angry all over again when she had married an actor who was a Catholic to boot! Papa's family had never approved of Mama because she wasn't Catholic—she was a Norwegian Lutheran. Mama and Papa hadn't cared what their families thought, or anyone else, though. They had loved each other.

Rosa switched the little bag of ice back to her left eye, wishing Mama would go on out of the bathroom and leave her alone. But she knew that it wouldn't happen. Mama was all the way in, now, and her eyes were still focused on Rosa's face.

"Maybe you should take a cold bath tomorrow morning. I heard somewhere that the mothers of the old-time child stars would do that sometimes. Give the kids a really chilly bath to make them wake up and shine."

Rosa shook her head. "I don't want a cold bath, Mama. I'm going to shine without that."

"Promise me you will," Mama said in a babyish singsong she used sometimes, as if Rosa were still little.

Rosa nodded. She would shine. Or she would try. Mama didn't need to make her promise. To prove it, Rosa smiled as widely and brightly as she could: a stage smile.

Mama laughed, her eyes lighting up. "Wonderful, sweetheart. No girl in this town is prettier or more talented than you are. You are my daughter, after all." Mama laughed at her own little joke, but Rosa knew what she wanted to hear.

"You're the one who should be going to casting calls and auditions," Rosa said dutifully.

Mama smiled, her dimples showing prettily. "Oh, no, not me. I am far too old."

"But you look so young," Rosa said, knowing exactly what Mama needed her to say. And it wasn't a lie. Mama looked like she was twenty-five, not almost thirty-five.

Mama smiled again. "Thank you, sweeties, but you are the real talent in this family." She reached out and patted the curlers. "I know you will take this town by storm one of these days soon."

"What if I don't?" Rosa blinked, not believing that she had said it aloud.

Mama reacted instantly, taking Rosa's hands in hers. "Of course you will. You are the prettiest and the most talented at every single audition and casting call.

I can't believe no one has seen in you what I see," she said, lowering her voice. "But they will. You are just a walking bundle of talent. A bundle. After all, you're my daughter!" she finished, laughing as though it were a joke that they shared, that only the two of them in the whole world could ever understand.

"And Papa's," Rosa breathed, not expecting her mother to hear, but she did.

"And your father's, of course. He was a great actor. He would have played leads if he had lived. Now, let's eat," Mama said, finally turning to go out the door. "And tomorrow I will leave my window shade up. We'll make breakfast early so your stomach will have plenty of time to settle before . . . " Mama hesitated, and Rosa smiled at her.

"Before we go to Paramount for the audition."

"Yes," Mama agreed, smiling back as though they were discussing how beautiful the weather had been, not the disgusting mess she had made once by throwing up while they had stood in line waiting for their turn. She had been sick other times, too, but she had always made it to the bathroom.

Mama had pushed an ice-cream sundae on her that day—when the auditions were set back a few hours—"to keep her energy up." The only thing that had come up was the sundae, chocolate sauce and all. All the other girls had turned away, pale-faced. Rosa knew that their stomachs were jumping, too, and they were afraid they'd be next. The mothers had hovered like clucking hens.

There were a lot of sisters at the extras auditions, especially for big films. The mothers wanted to hedge the bet. If they brought the whole family, the directors could pick and choose whichever of their children fit the age group.

Rosa felt guilty sometimes. Her mother only had one daughter to work with—a nervous, dark-haired, dark-eyed one who wasn't sure she would ever make it past the extras.

"Rosita, you can take the curlers out now," Mama said. "And call me when it's time to come look."

As her mother went out, closing the door, Rosa drew in a deep breath and set the little ice bag on the edge of the sink. Then she put on a bright smile and looked back into the mirror. She did look sort of sickly this morning. Directors mostly wanted kids who seemed healthy and plucky—kids who could work an all-day shoot and still stay on their feet and alert if there was night work to be done afterward.

Rosa picked up the soap. Clean, clean, clean, Mama always said. Kids who wanted to be stars had to be squeaky clean. Rosa washed her face and neck, then patted dry with a towel. She popped back the little hinged flap of one of her curlers and gently pulled it out of her hair. Her scalp itched furiously where the metal had been a moment before. She blinked and pulled out a second roller, then a third and a fourth. On the fifth, she began to cry quietly, tears soaking her cheeks.

"Mama?" Rosa called out, sniffling, hearing panic in her own voice. "Mama?"

CHAPTER TWO

"Oh, my heavens," Mama kept saying, over and over again. "Honey, how could it not curl in thirty hours? No, it was more like thirty-six hours, wasn't it? Because I got up so late?"

Rosa shook her head sadly without answering, staring into the mirror at her mother's face. Their eyes met in the reflection. Mama looked so bleak, so devastated, that Rosa ducked her chin, breaking the connection. "I'm sorry, Mama."

"Did you take them out last night?"

Rosa shook her head.

"Not even for a minute?"

Rosa shook her head again. The tendrils of nearly straight hair that sprang out from her head in stiff, silly arches swung against her cheeks, brushing the corners of her mouth. She pushed the hair away, irritated at the prickling tickle on her lips.

Mama was pulling in deep breaths. "Well, this will never do. Straight is better than this."

"We can just wash it again and—" Rosa began, but her mother interrupted her.

"But you *need* curls, sweeties. No one gets discovered without curls since Miss Temple came to town."

Rosa blinked back tears. Her hair was wrong. It had always been wrong, really, except for the bit parts she seemed to always end up with: the starving orphan peeking out of an alley; the poor waif beside the road; the girl-thief grabbing at a loaf of bread from an innocent farmer's wagon. And her face was wrong. Why couldn't Mama see that? Only the blond, pale-skinned kids got the plum parts. Even Jackie Coogan, the boy wonder of crying on cue. He was tragic in nearly every movie, his pale skin shining under the spots.

"Mama, maybe I can just get an extra part tomorrow," Rosa began. "That's fifteen dollars a week or even more, and that would be enough to—"

"Nonsense," her mother cut her off. "That kind of thinking is what holds you back, Rosa. I don't look at it that way, and I don't want you to, either. You've done extra work since before you could walk. It's time to shine."

Mama said the last word in a way that made her own face and eyes light up, her perfectly plucked brows lifting into twin arcs that climbed a full inch up her forehead. It was the kind of expression that vaudevillians used on the stage, so even the back row could see that they were excited and confident.

"So, no more bad-luck thoughts," Mama said evenly, her voice light, as though she were cajoling a baby. She put her hands on Rosa's shoulders and looked at her in the mirror again. "This is the day to be my best little girl and to do everything I say and maybe we will be discovered. You never know."

Rosa lowered her eyes back to her own image in the mirror. With her hair draping in limp curves around her face, it was hard to be as cheerful as Mama wanted her to be.

"All right?" Mama insisted, still using her babyish, singsong voice.

Rosa nodded.

Somewhere out on the street a car honked. Rosa glanced out the window. On Sundays, there was virtually no traffic on Las Palmas. Most of their neighbors walked to church or Mass or synagogue, so the enclosed court was quiet, none of the usual shouts of kids playing under the shaggy old palm trees.

Mama was humming. When she stopped, she smiled. "I have an idea for what we can do with that hair of yours. We have scads of time to figure this out, after all." She waved one hand airily as if the failure of the curlers was not a setback worth worrying about. "You get breakfast started. I'm going to make a phone call." Rosa nodded and tried to smile as her mother whirled around and went out.

The kitchen linoleum was chilly on the soles of Rosa's bare feet. She knew Mama would insist she put on slippers the instant she noticed, but until then, the cool smoothness of the floor felt good.

Rosa got down the bag of oatmeal. They ate it for breakfast morning after morning, summer and winter, whether they rose in the dark or, like today, closer to noon. Mama had been raised on oatmeal and was convinced it was what kept her complexion the envy of all her friends. Rosa thought it was more likely the result of the constant layer of cold cream she kept on her skin when they were at home. But there was no talking Mama out of her daily bowl of oatmeal. Besides, Rosa knew, it was cheap.

Mama and Mr. Green—the owner of the grocery store on the corner two blocks down—had a running argument going. He said that people preferred the rolled oats and that Mama had better get used to them before he had to quit selling the coarse-cut kind she preferred. Mama always arched her brows and twinkled at him, flirting just a little. He would always laugh, and there was always a bag or two of coarse oats on the bottom shelf when they needed more.

Rosa filled the oatmeal pan with water and set it on the stove, twisting the lever to turn on the current. A roach skittled across the counter, and she used the flyswatter to smash it, then threw it in the trash. She and Mama were clean, but the neighbors weren't so good about keeping their food in containers and off the table at night. The roaches came through the walls.

Other than the roaches, this place was as nice as anywhere she and Mama had lived since Papa had died. It was all right. Rosa liked the Hotpoint stove and the nice green sink. The plumbing was older than the appliances, but everything worked.

Rosa heard her mother dialing the phone. Then there was a silence. Rosa tiptoed to the door of the kitchen and held very still, trying not to breathe, so she could hear. But Mama's soft voice didn't carry well, and although Rosa could tell she was talking to a woman—Mama's voice got lower and slower when she spoke with men—she couldn't tell anything else.

Rosa took another step into the hall, leaning forward to catch even a few words of her mother's conversation. A roiling sound from the kitchen startled her, and she turned, flushing in embarrassment when she saw it was only the water, coming to a boil.

Rosa salted the water, then put in two fistfuls of the oats. She glanced at the door, hoping Mama wouldn't appear to scold her. Mama measured oats and flour by the handful, too, but she always said it wasn't proper and that she was trying to teach Rosa to do better than what she did herself.

Rosa stirred the oatmeal, then turned to peel

and core an apple. She cut it into fine pieces and put them in with the oatmeal. They were out of cinnamon, and it was a luxury they would have to do without until she found some kind of steady work again. Her last picture had needed crowds of kids in almost every scene. She earned her extra's wage for nearly six weeks. With what Mama brought in, it had been wonderful. But the gravy train of steady money had stopped when the movie was finished.

Still trying to listen to Mama, Rosa turned the stove burner down to its lowest setting. Then she turned back toward the door. She could hear her mother talking in a low, urgent voice, but the words blurred.

Rosa did a quick shuffle and step, her bare feet making a swishing rhythm on the linoleum. She whirled, then went back the other way, dancing her way, barefoot, through a soft-shoe routine she had learned for a film she had gotten extra work in earlier in the summer. She loved dancing. It was fun to perform with Mrs. Meglin's Famous Kiddies at department stores and old people's homes and wherever they got hired. But she loved dancing best when no one was watching.

Rosa whirled and swished her way back toward the stove, ending up with a dramatic swirl of her losers-weepers robe, one hand extended in a graceful gesture as she grabbed the oatmeal spoon and fell back to stirring like an actress in a musical, letting the rhythm of the music inside her mind time her movements.

Rosa daydreamed as she stood swaying to her internal orchestra, crumbling the brown sugar over the steaming oats. Even though she was imagining herself in a translucent blue gown, spinning across a dance floor while her proud fiancé looked on, she was careful not to put on too much. A pinch, Mama said, no more, ever—sugar rotted teeth—and a pretty smile was stock-in-trade for an actress.

By the time Rosa was carrying the bowls to the table, her daydream had shifted. Now she was in an endless library, happily lost, and not even Mama could find her.

Rosa crossed back to the sink, wondering what it would be like to be a star like Mary Pickford had been, living in a mansion with a handsome actor for her husband, rich enough to do anything she wanted. When Mary Pickford and Douglas Fairbanks, had driven down Sunset Boulevard, people would hit their brakes and pull their automobiles over to stare.

Rosa had seen her a number of times from a distance. She had been unable to do anything but stare at the lovely face of the woman who had begun as a fairy star, acting while she was still just a baby. Back then, she had been known as Baby Gladys. She had changed her name to Mary much later so people would see her as a woman and directors would hire her again.

Mama sometimes reminded Rosa that Mary Pickford idolized her own mother and had often been quoted in the papers crediting her mother with her success. Mary was unusual, Rosa knew that much. She had started in silent films, then made it into the talkies. She had kept her audience as she had grown up. Most of the child stars of the twenties had become has-beens by the time they were nine or ten.

Rosa turned to face the door again. Mama was *still* talking. Rosa knew she was trying to talk someone into something, from the wheedling, sweet tone of her voice. And it was definitely a woman—Mama never would have let herself sound that whiny and pitiful to a man.

Rosa slumped into the chair in front of her bowl. While she had been waltzing around the kitchen, pretending the linoleum was a ballroom set, Mama had been cooking up something much worse than oatmeal, she was sure. But what? She had said she wanted to get a new arrangement of Rosa's sheet music. Rosa wanted to work out a new routine altogether soon. *March of the Toys* was a baby's score, even if it was anew, hot song and the Laurel and Hardy movie it had come from had been a hit The little soldier outfit she danced in was too babyish. Mama had let it out two or three times already. All the mothers made costumes like that, with wide seam allowances that could be adjusted as their children grew.

Mechanically lifting her spoon and listening to the intermittent murmur of Mama's voice coming down the hall and through the kitchen door, Rosa began to eat. They had a rule: If one of them couldn't come to the table, the other one was to eat her food while it was hot.

It was almost always Mama who didn't make it on time, of course. She was often out working. But even when she was home, she was on the phone a lot, keeping track of studio dates—or sitting in Papa's old chair by the living room window, going through the classified ads. Rosa thought Mama should audition for bit parts, but she never would.

Rosa had the spoon halfway to her mouth when she heard her mother place the phone receiver back in the cradle. She set the spoon down and held her breath. Her mother was humming. Rosa felt her stomach tightening. She reached up and fingered a lank, barely curled strand of her hair just as her mother came swinging through the doorway. "Who was that?"

"On the phone?" Mama teased.

Rosa frowned at her. "Mama, just tell me who it was. Was it about . . . " Rosa held up a strand of her hair.

Mama's face lit up, and she nodded, touching her own hair in a mirror-reversed gesture. "You guessed it, sweeties. Monique is going to help us out if we can get there before the place opens tomorrow morning. We have to get up around four, though."

Rosa blinked, but Mama just patted her cheek and smiled. "Don't you worry. Monique is one of the best. She used to work up on Hollywood Boulevard, you know, in one of those expensive beauty parlors. You'll see, she'll do it just fine."

CHAPTER THREE

Rosa stood in front of the mirror while Mama cleaned up the kitchen. That was another rule: Mama cleaned up if Rosa cooked, and vice versa. Usually, Rosa loved the time when Mama was cleaning up, because she could daydream or fiddle around, or sneak outside to see the kids who lived around the court. She hadn't had time to make a real friend since Callie had moved away.

The apartments were small and not very pretty—but the garden in the center of the shabby u-shaped building was wonderful. It was old, with tall palms and giant philodendrons. There were fan palms, too, in clumps. The older boys would cut the barbed stems to use as play swords, wrapping the bases in old cloth to make handles—until someone's parents saw them and took the spiked palm fronds away.

Today, Rosa thought, her little bit of free time was too tiny to be worth savoring. Looking into the mirror, she felt almost sick. Her hair really did look silly. It wasn't curled or even waved, it was just *poofed* out from her head. She turned on the water faucet and went to work, wetting it thoroughly and pulling the comb through it over and over until it lay close to her head again as it usually did. Then she braided it and went to her closet. She had thirteen different costumes, and three dresses for everyday: blue, pink, yellow. She put on her yellow dress and paused in front of her mirror on the way out. Her hair looked normal again, and she smiled at herself.

Rosa ventured back out into the living room. She could hear her mother singing in her own bedroom, her voice low and sultry. Rosa stood still, listening. Mama really did have a nice voice. As good as most stars' voices, or even better.

"Mama?" Rosa called at the end of the song. "Can I go outside and see who's around?"

"Oh, sweeties, no," Mama called back, her voice breathless and startled-sounding. "Not today. Today we have to get your sheet music replaced, and I thought it would be a good idea to go by the studio and pick up a class."

Rosa sighed. "I went four times last week."

"A little extra can't hurt. And if the bigger girls aren't scheduled too close, I thought you could do a run-through."

"A run-through," Rosa whispered in time with her mother's last few words. She had forgotten the sheet music errand, but a full class and then a run-through were the last things she wanted to do today. Especially not with Miss Franklin, the weekend teacher. Miss Franklin was so critical. She had started as a part-time teacher, running classes on Saturday and Sunday, when Miss Gavin took time off.

Mama got dressed and came striding out. As usual, Rosa stared at her for a few seconds, wondering how they could be related. Her mother's hair was blond, soft, and curly, and she was tall and thin. But it was much more than that. Her mother was graceful, elegant. Standing in the doorway in her ashes-of-rose dress, she looked as stunning as any actress could ever have looked. The bias-cut skirt draped across her flat belly and hips and fell to mid-calf. The little sweater she had put on over the fitted bodice was clinging to her shoulders, making her look as slim as a teenager. But much more polished.

"Whatever are you staring at?" Mama demanded.

Rosa shook her head. "You look beautiful. I will never look like that," she added very quietly.

"No," her mother said sharply, "you won't. You will be a little smaller, I think, with beautiful smooth skin and shining dark hair and your pretty flashing brown eyes. And you will have your very own flair and style. You don't need to wish you could look like anyone else."

Mama sounded so sure that Rosa had to smile. "Do you really think so, Mama?"

"I do. And I believe you will be an important actress someday, too, Rosa. A star."

The way Mama said the word "star" was as though she was talking about getting into heaven. Rosa looked into her eyes for a moment, then had to look away. She glanced down at her yellow dress, at the wide sash that she had tied by reaching behind herself. It was probably a wilted wad of fabric in back. She reached around to retie it.

"Want me to do it, sweeties?" Mama asked.

Rosa nodded, and her mother turned her around. In a few deft movements, the bow was done and there was no doubt in Rosa's mind that it was even, flounced, and perfect.

"Woolworth's first," Mama announced, "but get your tap box."

Rosa turned back to her room. Her dance things were always packed. The cardboard box had a shiny drawing of Betty Boop on the top and a satin cord fixed to the lid. Rosa picked it up. It swung lightly from her hand, and as they went out the front door, Rosa was struck by the thought that most of the time, when she left the front door with Mama, she was carrying this box. She had carried containers like it her whole life.

"You look glum," Mama said, reaching into her purse for a stick of chewing gum. She offered one to Rosa, but Rosa refused politely. She had read somewhere that Mary Pickford thought women chewing gum looked like cows chewing their cuds. The image was so repugnant, she hadn't really enjoyed a piece of spearmint since.

"Keep up, sweeties," Mama said over her shoulder as she turned down the garden walk and headed for the street, her high heels clicking on the red tiles.

Rosa heard giggles as they passed the thick clump of bougainvillea that draped the stuccoed wall at the entrance to the court. There was a fort beneath the giant, thorned vine. Kids had dug out little rooms, burrowing through the dense plant a little at a time. One girl said that her father remembered playing in the bougainvillea fort when he was a kid. Rosa wasn't sure it was true. The little girl was an actress—she went to as many auditions as Rosa did herself—and she loved to make up far-fetched stories.

Rosa glanced toward the giggles as she passed the house-sized mound of the vine, but she couldn't see anyone's face through the thick crop of bright red leaves that framed the vine's tiny white flowers.

"Come on," Mama called back again, and Rosa ran two or three steps to catch up, her tap box banging against her leg.

As her mother clicked down the hot, sunny sidewalk, Rosa found herself lagging behind. Mama kept turning, then stopping to wait. "You are the slowpoke today," she said, finally slowing her step a little. "Are you tired?"

Rosa nodded, then shook her head. "Not really. I just wish we could go to a movie or something."

"But we have too many other things to get done today. And tomorrow—"

"I know," Rosa interrupted her mother quietly. She didn't want to hear about how she needed to prepare for the audition. Did Mama really think she forgot every ten minutes that it was coming up and that it was important? She imagined the cool, thick carpets inside the Pantages Theater. There was a wonderful double-railed brass banister that she had slid down twice when the ushers weren't looking. She and Callie, who had moved back to Ohio after a few months of not getting movie parts. Her parents had given up.

Rosa glanced up. Mama was walking with her eyes straight ahead now, and Rosa was grateful. Somewhere across the street a man wolf-whistled, and Rosa saw her mother give him a nearly imperceptible nod acknowledging the compliment politely but without giving him any encouragement at all.

As they turned the corner, walking past fifteen or twenty tall palms growing in a curving line, Rosa looked up at the Hollywoodland sign. mama said it was the work of some real estate agent, trying to sell land. Rosa tried to imagine the hill without the sign and couldn't. She loved it, especially at night when the letters were lit up by the light bulbs that outlined them. She had read in a tourist pamphlet that the letters were fifty feet high. Fifty feet! No wonder people could read the sign for miles.

But how many people had come to hate that sign and everything it stood for? she wondered. Callie's mother had said she detested it. She had spent all her savings to bring Callie to California, and then they had had to go home to Ohio without any money left to start over with.

Rosa glanced at her mother again. Mama had said she felt sorry for Callie because she had had to leave. Rosa wondered if Callie was sorry, or if she was happier now. She had hated practicing all the time and she hadn't really liked performing very much, anyway. She had cried before auditions

Woolworth's storefront was red andthe letters of the sign were gold. Mama strode along the sidewalk, passing the crowded windows with their displays of toys, cloth, lunch pails, cosmetics, and nearly everything else anyone would ever want to buy or to own.

When Mama slowed before one of the pairs of propped-open double doors and then turned sharply to go inside, Rosa stepped from the scalding sun into deep, cool shade as they crossed the threshold.

Inside the big store the sound of the pianist tinkling her way out of one of her quick-cadence marching tunes made Rosa smile. It was the usual elderly woman today, her white hair well groomed and her heavyset body dwarfing the bench. Rosa could hear the odd echoing sound of her own footsteps and she inhaled the familiar dusty smell of the store, wrinkling her nose and smiling. Rosa liked Woolworth's, and she loved looking around at the thousands of things for sale here.

"Don't touch anything," Mama reminded her.

Rosa nodded automatically. It was hard to keep her hands by her sides. The golden, polished floor seemed to stretch forever in every direction, and the bright merchandise beckoned her. Rosa squeezed her sun-dazzled eyes shut, then opened them again and found she could see better. The store was quiet. Woolworth's was not very crowded today. Perfect.

"Want a sandwich or something?" Mama asked as they passed the first huge oval-shaped counter. The pianist wound up her march, then segued into a show tune that Rosa recognized vaguely from an old movie.

"Sure," Rosa answered, staring at the clerk they were passing. She looked sleepy—all but her jaw. She was chewing her gum a mile a minute, blinking slowly as she looked to make sure no one in her department needed help choosing a hair bow or a set of shoelaces from the hundreds of choices in the glass-fronted cases. Mama always said working in Woolworth's was the kind of job girls got if they had no other choice. They couldn't live off their dime-an-hour wage, and there was little hope of a raise. Most of them were girls who still lived with their parents.

Mama stopped a moment at the next counter, looking at bottles of perfume. Rosa stopped, too, searching for something that interested her while Mama leaned on the polished wood of the counter and waited for the department clerk to notice her.

There were goldfish swimming lazily in wide bowls lined up on a shelf in the next department. Rosa drifted away from her mother. She walked slowly, staring. The beautiful fish shone like coins in the water, their sides silvery beneath the deep orange-gold. Watching them, Rosa suddenly felt sad. They were going in circles, every one of them. Swimming and swimming and only ending up back where they had started.

"Oh, never mind," Mama said suddenly and loudly enough for Rosa to look up sharply. One older woman frowned at Mama over her handful of stocking packages, then half-turned to go back to her shopping. Rosa saw the source of Mama's irritation instantly. The perfume clerk was busy with someone else, and Mama had gotten tired of waiting.

Leading the way, Mama clicked over the bright oak floor and didn't so much as pause again until they were standing in front of the soda fountain, staring at the big pictures of the food. Rosa knew what she wanted. She always got the same thing. It was Mama who had a decision to make.

Rosa let her eyes drift over the posters, taking in the colorful portraits of the ham sandwich and the open-faced turkey with its perfect mound of cole slaw. She stared at the rows of inverted soda glasses while Mama gave the counter boy their order.

Then they climbed up and sat on the high stools. They were wide and flat on top, not really comfortable, but it didn't matter. The fun part was swiveling them back and forth, thinking up reasons to push her foot against the counter to turn herself, looking one way, then the other.

What Rosa really wanted to do was spin all the way around to see how fast she could make the stool whirl, but she knew Mama would never stand for it. Besides, she was too old for anyone to smile at her tolerantly and think such behavior was cute.

When the fountain attendant brought them their cherry Cokes, Rosa jumped down to go get straws out of the covered jar. She reached in politely and tried to touch only the two straws she was taking. Climbing back up, she handed Mama a straw, then settled in herself, pulling the curved glass toward herself. The chipped ice was always beautiful to her, catching the light like diamonds. The straw's waxy paper felt smooth against her lips as she sipped her soda, closing her eyes happily. The soda jerk had gotten it just right this time—not too much cherry flavoring.

"So one run-through will be enough, you think?" Mama asked.

Rosa's aimless thoughts were forced aside. "I wasn't even thinking about it, Mama."

Mama looked peeved. "Well, I think you had better start, don't you?"

Rosa looked down. "One run-through will be enough."

Mama waited until Rosa looked up, and was staring at her when she did. "This is very, very important, Rosa."

"I know that, Mama." Rosa held her mother's gaze, knowing that she would really be in for a lecture if she looked aside or acted like she wasn't taking things seriously enough.

"One run-through is enough? I have the money to pay for studio time if you think you need more."

"You do?" Rosa was surprised. Mama had not had a full day of work in a week.

"I saved a little out of your last two weeks at Fox," Mama told her. "I look ahead when I can. You know that."

"Here we are," the counter boy announced, and Rosa looked up, startled, moving her hands so the plates could be set in front of them. Mama's club sandwich looked good. Her own tuna on toast looked perfect as always.

They ate in silence, and Rosa was glad. The slices of sweet pickle were delicious, and she ate them first, as always, then her handful of potato chips. Only when they were gone did she lift the triangle of her sandwich. The tuna salad was delicious, the toasted bread crunchy but not too crunchy.

Mama let the whole meal pass without saying another word about the audition. She smiled and paid the ticket, then gestured for Rosa to get down from the stool, turning to lead the way back through the maze of oblong counters.

In the music department, Mama walked down the rows of waist-high racks like a prowling cat. She usually looked over the selection carefully—they both did. Rosa loved to pull out the folded sheets of music, poring over the cover art. There were silhouettes of lovers dancing, detailed drawings of toys and ships and carnivals and anything else a song could be about. The best-sellers usually had pictures of dolled-up actors and actresses pretending to gaze into each other's eyes.

But this time, Rosa had to walk fast to keep up with Mama, her eyes barely managing to catch the lines of advertising that leapt out in bold, slanted print and bright colors as she passed. Each one claimed to hold the hottest new tune from a hit movie.

"Here it is," Mama announced as she pulled a copy of *March of the Toys* from the rack. Rosa nodded and turned immediately. Mama would think she wasn't concentrating on what was important if she acted like she wanted to spend precious time browsing music they weren't going to buy.

Mama pointed, and they made their way back to the front of the store. As they sat through the pianist's heavy-handed rendition of the arrangement, Rosa had to admit her mother was right. This version of her routine theme was better than the one she had been using.

"Hear anything that would trip you up?" Mama asked when the gray-haired woman handed them back the folded sheet music.

Rosa shook her head.

"Maybe it isn't so smart to change arrangements the day before," Mama said.

"It's fine, Mama," Rosa reassured her. "And I'll have the run-through to see if there are hitches."

Mama beamed. "That's my girl. You are a great little trouper, Rosa."

Rosa looked up into her mother's face, feeling her cheeks flush at Mama's compliment.

"And you are going to be a star," Mama added. "My little girl, a great big star."

Rosa saw the urgency in her mother's eyes and forced herself to keep smiling.

CHAPTER FOUR

The studio was only five blocks from Woolworth's. Rosa had been silent for most of the way, but Mama didn't seem to notice. She was humming, then whistling softly, still walking fast along the sidewalk. It was almost three in the afternoon, Rosa saw, passing a barbershop with a wall clock she could read through the glass. The streets were pretty much deserted—everyone had gone home after church.

By the time they turned onto Gordon Street, and Rosa saw the little knot of girls carrying boxes just like hers, she slowed down without meaning to, dragging her feet. She didn't want to go to a lesson. She didn't even really want to go to a movie. What she longed to do today was spend a few hours in the library. She was so tired of being nervous, of practicing and thinking about how to became a star.

The cool silence of the children's book section of the library always felt special and sacred to Rosa—sort of like church. It calmed herheart. And then there was Miss Campbell. The tall, willowy librarian was always there to help, then gone again just as quickly to let her open each book entirely alone.

Rosa loved good stories. Some of her own were sort of good, she thought. Or they could be if she worked harder at writing them. "I want to go to the library," Rosa said aloud.

"But it's Sunday, sweeties," her mother answered without hesitation. "Maybe Wednesday or Thursday."

Rosa nodded, knowing her mother wouldn't turn to look at her, but feeling that she should respond, anyway. Wednesday or Thursday. It sounded like an eternity away from this morning, and Rosa knew all too well that when Mama said they would do something in a few days, they often never did it at all.

"Rosa!" Mama said, her voice stern.

Startled, Rosa looked up. She had stopped on the steps without realizing it. "I'm coming, Mama."

"Class starts in five minutes, Miss Franklin says. You need to get changed." Mama had her hands on her hips and she was frowning. "What's the matter with you?"

Rosa shrugged and looked up the steps. Standing not far behind Mama was the teacher herself. She had on makeup like she was about to go on a stage. And she was smoking, the cigarette dangling languidly from her fingers. Her right cheek sported a drawn-on beauty mark. She was very thin.

"Rosa?" Mama insisted. "Is something the matter?"

Rosa met Mama's eyes. "Nothing. I'm nervous about tomorrow, I guess."

"Nonsense. You are going to sparkle." Mama gestured impatiently, and Rosa went up the steps toward her. At the top, Mama turned so they could walk together into the changing room.

The beginners' class was getting dressed to go home, and the intermediates were just straggling in. Rosa looked around, the squeals of the little girls grating on her nerves.

The benches were littered with stockings and hair bows and little cotton sweaters. Mothers scolded and cajoled and helped pick things up and put them in the dance class boxes. One or two of the girls had real dance gear. As always, Rosa felt a quick stab of jealousy when she saw the black leather bags and their spanking new tap shoes.

As the beginners dressed and left, the noise level slowly sank. Rosa got into her shorts and top as quickly as she could, turning her back to slide the top on over her head. Then she sat on the bench and pulled out her shoes. Out of long habit, she turned her right shoe over and checked the taps, toe first, then heel, then her left shoe.

In her very first class, when she had been four years old, a loose tap had tripped a girl up and she had fallen—with everyone laughing because she clawed at the air like an old-fashioned vaudeville windmill move—then sat down, hard. Rosa had vowed she would never let that happen to her.

Wriggling her feet into her tap shoes, Rosa tied the wide straps of grosgrain ribbon tightly over her insteps. These were not the shoes she would be wearing tomorrow. For auditions she used a second pair, the exact same size and fit but with fresher ribbons and much less wear. Her mother had insisted on spending the extra money.

Rosa stood up in her taps and looked around the dressing room again. All the little girls were gone. But even the intermediates looked young to her. She was the tallest girl in the room.

Rosa frowned. Mama didn't want her to move up into the classes for older girls, because she said that they learned a different, more mature style—something that was a mistake for Rosa to spend time learning. She said that all the new talent in Hollywood started young—the younger the better. That was why they had to hurry up and get her discovered.

Rosa knew it was true. At eleven and a half, she was often one of the oldest girls at the auditions now, too. Most of the girls her age and older put on slinky dresses and makeup and tried to look like college girls so they could get adult roles in movies.

"Psst! Rosa?"

She looked up. "What?"

Mama was standing in the doorway. "I got it all arranged with the piano lady. It isn't the regular one, it's someone they just hire for weekends but—" Mama stopped midsentence as the strains of a quick-time waltz tune burst from the piano. It was the signal that the teacher was ready for them.

Every girl in the dressing room stood up and filed out. Rosa brought up the end of the line. Other mothers, not just her own, were in the anteroom, and they all seemed to have something to say as their daughters passed them. Mama leaned forward and whispered, "Stand straight and smile. Be the prettiest in the room!"

Rosa nodded, but somewhere deep in her stomach a knot tightened. She walked into the dance studio watching herself in the mirrors that covered the walls, striding along with her chin held unnaturally high, her steps measured and graceful, like a beauty pageant contestant.

"Tallest to shortest, starting on the right," Miss Franklin announced in a shrill voice.

Rosa stared at her. The new weekend teacher was pretty, maybe even beautiful, but she spoiled her own looks with her air of impatient boredom. She stood flat-footed with her hands on her hips. Her crimson-painted mouth was pursed as though girls were particularly distasteful creatures, and that here, by some unfair and nasty surprise, she found herself in a roomful of them.

"By height," she called out as though addressing people whose ears and brains were not connected. "Line. Up. By. Height."

Rosa simply moved to the tall end and took her place. Then, as the others milled around sorting themselves out, she stared into the mirrors that covered two walls of the studio. She corrected her posture, lifting her chin without tilting her head, then tilting it slightly and gauging the effect.

Once the others had finally worked out their hierarchy, Miss Franklin gave them a tiny curtsy. The whole line of girls sank, then rose, curtsying back.

"To the barre, please, girls," Miss Franklin called out, pitching her voice at the same shrill, high tone as before.

Rosa stepped up to the barre and followed the commands, aware that her mother, standing with all the others, was peeking into the studio door, watching.

Rosa tried to relax. Usually she enjoyed the stretching exercises that would warm her up to dance. She extended her left leg, placing her foot on top of the barre. Then, following Miss Franklin's counted pattern, she leaned to the side, touching her forehead to her elevated knee. Then she arched back, curving one hand over her head.

Switching sides, they repeated the exercises,

then began another set, each time leaning backward farther and farther, loosening their backs for back-bends and their legs for splits. A girl who could do splits well was always applauded, Mama said, because it looks so impossible to anyone who didn't dance. It looked like it should *hurt*.

"Follow the music now. Begin with a basic time step," Miss Franklin ordered.

Rosa and the other girls fell into the easy tap-shuffle rhythm that allowed them to stay with the beat in a four-square rhythm.

"Now soft shoe and segue into the Charleston, beginning now, four bars each step, and begin, two, three, four, and there you are, that's good," she called out, and the line switched to the once popular dance that had become part of every dancer's repertoire.

"And backward drag and two, three, four, and, windmill . . . keep your arms high, make it look high and wide and spectacular," Miss Franklin instructed. "Reach!"

The class went by as though Rosa were under-water. Miss Franklin's counting was true and steady, and Rosa knew the dance shorthand that all perform-ers learned if they worked as extras long enough.

Rosa glanced over to see her mother grinning at her, and knew it was her signal to smile wider. She obeyed the cue without thinking.

"Look pretty," Miss Franklin demanded suddenly,

and Rosa knew she had noticed her reaction to Mama's prompt. Every girl in the class smiled brightly as though this were the most amazingly wonderful time she had ever had in her life.

Rosa turned on her sparkle, too, as Mama always described it. But then she found herself wondering why, at a class, it was so important to pretend to be thrilled to be able to do steps she had learned how to do when she was seven years old.

The first routine finally ended, and the girls came to an uneven stop. Rosa was a little out of breath, but not tired. She just wanted the rest of the lesson to be over so she could do her run-through for Mama and be finished until tomorrow.

The thought of the big audition unsettled her enough that she missed a cue, and Miss Franklin stopped everyone to turn and stare at Rosa. "Daydreaming?"

Rosa felt herself blushing. "No, Miss Franklin."

"What do they call it where you come from, then?" she demanded, and the other girls laughed softly, an uncomfortable sound.

"All right, girls," the teacher said loudly, signaling that the girls could now take their embarrassing attention off Rosa. "Let's start again." The line began to move again. This time Rosa was careful to keep her concentration.

When the lesson finally ended, Mama came in

to hug her and tell her how great she had looked. Rosa could hear the other mothers saying the same thing to their daughters, every one of them with complete faith in her eyes. Each and every one believed that her child would be a star.

Mama gave Rosa ten minutes to rest after class. Then she handed the glossy new sheet music to the pianist. The woman marched into the introduction the way she had marched into every song all afternoon long, with effort and exactness.

Rosa asked her to play the arrangement once, straight through, exactly as it was on the page. She was warmed up and loose muscled after the lesson, so the second time through, she simply danced her routine, ending with the Russian splits her mother thought would knock the executives' eyes out. She held her closing pose for a full fifteen seconds, counting chimpanzees slowly, as her mother always insisted on her doing. Then she kept her toes pointed and swung her left leg around to lie parallel with her right. Only then did she bend her knees, toes still pointed, her back as straight as anything. She rose gracefully and stood still again, her hands behind her back, grinning like a fool at the empty, mirrored reflection of herself on the far wall.

"I was thinking today that you should be going to Lawlor," Mama said as Rosa came out of the studio, her hair damp with sweat.

"Really?" Rosa looked at her mother. Lawlor was where the show kids all went to school. Mrs. Lawlor understood that six weeks of location shooting was bound to interrupt learning adverbs and pronouns, and that was all right. Mickey Rooney and all the great kid stars had been going there forever. And there were up-and-coming kids, too. The youngest Gumm sister was there, Rosa knew. Everyone had heard of her amazing voice. Baby Gumm had changed her stage name to Judy Garland, Rosa had heard. She had often daydreamed about what she would do if some studio asked her to change her name. She didn't want to. Papa wouldn't want her to.

"Lawlor would be great for you," Mama was saying.

Rosa could only nod. When the Lawlor kids put on their annual school shows at the Wilshire Ebell Theater, talent scouts went to look for new faces in the cast.

Rosa looked into her mother's face, her heart lifting with excitement. "Do you mean it? Could we afford it?"

Mama waved away the question with an airy breeze of her hand. "Once you are a star, sweeties, there won't be anything we can't afford."

Rosa nodded numbly, wondering why in the world she had thought her mother would respond in any other way. Of course it depended on her being discovered. Everything did.

CHAPTER FIVE

For Monday morning, Mama had borrowed an alarm clock from the woman next door—but then she put it next to Rosa's bed, not her own. So when it went off, clanging like a midnight fire engine, Rosa was the one who sat bolt upright, her heart pounding in the darkness.

She reached out as her senses began to function, and hit the switch to turn it off. In the sudden silence she lay back down, her pulse still racketing inside her chest. Over her own quickened breathing she could hear Mrs. Carillo's roosters crowing.

The old woman had five or six of them—big, ugly ones with folded-over pink combs and long, curved spurs. Rosa listened to the hoarse, grating cries of the big birds. They competed, she was sure of it. Each one was bent on taking center stage and keeping it as long as possible.

After two or three minutes, Rosa sat up again. As much as she wanted to this morning, it was too late to play her not-moving game. She had already been sitting up, to turn off the alarm clock, so the rules had already been broken.

Rosa swung her feet to the floor and counted to twenty chimpanzees, waiting for her mind to clear enough so she knew she wouldn't bump into the walls going down the hall. Then she stood up and tiptoed into Mama's room.

She was tempted for an instant to lean down and shout to wake her mother—so they could share the same wild pulse rate this morning. But she didn't. Mama was grumpy if she was startled awake. That was why she had put the alarm in Rosa's bedroom in the first place.

"Mama?" Rosa whispered.

Her mother opened her eyes. "Give me five minutes, sweeties, and I am ready," she said in a groggy voice. Rosa went back to her own room to dress.

The sidewalks were still nearly empty, and the sun was just beginning to pop up when they went out the front door. Rosa felt as nervous as she had ever felt in her life. First Monique, then the audition.

"Stand up straight, shoulders way back, and lift that chin!" Mama said as they came out the door. Automatically, Rosa did exactly what her mother had told her to do, squaring her shoulders and arching her lower back just a little.

"Very good," Mama said softly as they started out.

Rosa dreaded audition days for a number of reasons, and Mama's near-constant advice was one of them. As they walked, Rosa led the way while Mama purposely fell back a dozen feet or so. Passing beneath a streetlamp, Rosa glanced back at her, earning a frown. She knew what Mama was doing. She'd get far enough behind Rosa to see if she was walking perfectly.

Rosa knew the way, so she just kept going, ignoring her mother's scrutiny from behind except to move her feet in a perfectly straight line, gliding along from step to step. She kept her shoulders back and her head held high.

Walking perfectly was something that Mama had drilled into her for so long that it came naturally, anyway. Sometimes she tried to slouch along like other kids did—and she really couldn't. Her back seemed to find its way back to being straight the minute she stopped thinking about it.

"Like someone leading a parade," Mama reminded Rosa from behind her, as though she had read her thoughts.

Rosa straightened her spine and let her steps come from her hips, gracefully, like a dancer's. She heard Mama make a little sound of approval from behind her, and she smiled a little as she followed the curving sidewalk to the left, then stepped off the curb to cross the street.

The little bungalow houses that lined the street were still mostly dark at this hour. Only here and there could Rosa see a lit window. In these hard times, no one burned lights without a good reason except rich people who just didn't care how much money they spent. That was certainly not the case in this neighborhood, Rosa knew. So if there were lights on, someone was up and getting dressed for work.

As they passed one of the lit windows, Rosa looked in to see an older woman crossing herself before a little framed picture of Jesus on the wall. "We should go to Mass next week," Rosa said. Mama shrugged. She had converted to Catholicism, but Rosa knew she didn't care all that much about the Church.

Another car went past. "Poor darlings," Rosa said aloud, using her Garbo voice. "Poor darlings who are so cooped up in their automobiles and who cannot enjoy the dawn air with us."

Mama laughed, and Rosa felt herself smiling.

"Do it again," Mama said.

Rosa cleared her throat and dropped her voice an octave, breathing out the words to imitate the familiar voice of Greta Garbo—a voice just about everyone in the whole world recognized after all the movies Garbo had made.

Mama took a few long strides and caught up, still laughing. "You've really gotten good at that one. Let me hear Lupe Velez."

Rosa pulled in a long breath and began chattering in quick tempo, accented English, reciting the up-and-coming comedienne's dialogue from *Hot Pepper*, her latest film.

Mama laughed aloud. "I loved that movie. That little woman should have done comedy from the start, not all those serious roles. She is going to make a mint."

Rosa let Mama go on about Lupe and how talented she was without interrupting her. Rosa knew the story already, of course. At the Meglin Kiddies rehearsals, the gossip was almost all about stars. And Mama had told her before, too. But Rosa was polite and let her mother retell it. It was pretty impressive.

At Miss Velez's first performance in Mexico, when the Actors' Guild wouldn't let her perform, she hadn't given up. Instead, she had met the audience as they came in, standing on a chair to explain why she couldn't get up on the stage to give the show.

Rosa imagined herself doing the same thing, and shivered a little even though it was warm out. Miss Velez was gutsy, all right. What if the audience had booed her? What if they had been so angry over the canceled performance that they hadn't let her talk at all? Rosa had seen people jeered and shouted right off stages in the vaudeville houses. The very idea of it made her stomach clench.

As Mama wound up the story, Rosa murmured and nodded so Mama would know she was listening—and wouldn't start over. Rosa knew that every time Mama brought up Miss Velez's name, or Dolores Del

Río's, or Ramon Navarro's, she was saying that golden-haired girls and boys were not the only ones to make it big in Hollywood.

After a few minutes, Mama fell into silence, and Rosa was careful not to say anything to start her talking again. The sound of their footsteps on the sidewalk was pleasant. Rosa shortened her stride slightly, changing the rhythm, timing her steps so her footfalls came a split second after her mother's. Then she speeded up until they came a second before, like two dancers, slightly off.

At the next corner, they turned right onto Fountain Street. The buildings here were mostly stores, not homes. The block was dark except for one light in the bakery at the end of the street. As they walked, Mama giggled suddenly and pointed straight upward. "What does that remind you of?"

Rosa looked up, trying to see what her mother had seen. After a moment, she lowered her eyes and shook her head. "It's just the sky, Mama. It's getting gray, and the stars are gone. . . . "

Rosa trailed off, hoping for a clue, but Mama didn't say anything for a long time. They passed under a streetlight, and Rosa could see that her mother's eyes were glistening.

"It's like being in one of our blanket tents," Mama said a moment later. She said it very softly, in a dreamy voice. "Remember?"

Rosa looked up again and smiled. "I remember, but Mama, you are so silly sometimes."

Her mother sighed. "I am not silly. Those are precious memories for me. Our rainy days." She sighed again, a long, wistful sound.

Mama's rainy day tents were something Rosa would never forget. Right after Papa had been killed, it had been rainy and gloomy for nearly two weeks. Everyone had said that the weather was freakish— that the city of Los Angeles never went that long without sunshine. Mama had said the sky was crying for Papa.

As they passed beneath the next streetlight, Rosa kicked at a pebble on the sidewalk and sent it spinning into the darkness. She had been five years old— really little. The funeral had been long, and so many people had been there that Rosa had gotten separated from Mama for a little while, and it had scared her. The cemetery was big—or it had seemed big then. Now, when they went to visit Papa's grave, it seemed much smaller.

"I can still see those tents we made," Mama said. "Clear as day. Like we had just taken them down this morning."

Rosa nodded. She could see them, too. When the dark, gloomy days were making them feel too terrible and they had cried all they could stand to cry, Mama had started making tents. It was time to get away from their dreary routines, she said, to take a vacation.

But they had no money to go anywhere, Rosa learned later. And it was still raining. So Mama had taken every bedspread and sheet and blanket in the house and had sewn the edges together in long, looping stitches. Then she had put in the leaf in their dining room table and used it for a flat center-beam. Draping the blankets over it, she had stuck the chairs under, too, moving them around to make different rooms beneath the blankets. The tent had filled the living room and spilled over into their little dining room and into the wide entry hall.

They had eaten dinner in their tent, slept in it, Mama dragging their mattresses beneath it, placing chairs under the canopy to form bedchambers for both of them. The tent had felt so safe to Rosa, and for the longest time, she expected her father to come home and push the door open, laughing when he saw what they had done to the neat living room of their house.

"Remember when it stopped raining?" Mama whispered as Rosa stepped from the curb to cross the street. "And we took it all apart?"

Rosa nodded, looking back at her mother over her shoulder. "I helped you cut the stitches loose."

Mama nodded. "You have always helped me, Rosa. You are the best daughter any mother could ever wish for."

Rosa smiled and turned away quickly. Mama would get all weepy now. They were almost there. "Do you see her car?" she asked, to distract her mother from any more sad stories.

Mama lifted her head as they stepped back onto the sidewalk. "No. She isn't there yet."

Rosa exhaled. Maybe Monique wouldn't show up. Maybe she had thought about what would happen to her if Mrs. Bert caught her working on Rosa before the shop opened for the day. She could lose her job, after all. It was a big favor that Mama had asked of her. Maybe Monique had decided to be sensible and would apologize later for standing them up.

"There," Mama said suddenly, bumping Rosa's shoulder with her own. "There she comes!"

Rosa swallowed hard. No doubt about it. It was Monique's ten-year-old Ford—missing the passenger side fender and door. Monique was saving up for a new car, but everyone was tight with money now, and her tips had dwindled down to almost nothing.

As the lopsided sedan parked in front of the flat-roofed little building that housed Mrs. Bert's Palace of Beauty, Rosa glanced at her mother. In the graying light, she could see Mama's eyes shining with grateful tears. "Monique is a saint," Mama said, meeting Rosa's eyes.

Rosa nodded, afraid to say anything at all. She shivered, waiting as Monique went through the little shop's front door. Rosa heard the radio squawk as Monique turned on the mood music that was always playing at the Palace of Beauty. Rosa glanced up at her mother. "Can we just go in?"

Mama frowned. "I don't know, sweeties. But you should say 'may I,' not 'can I.'"

"May I, then?" Rosa asked. "May we?"

"Wait," Mama said. "Wait until she sees us."

Rosa held her breath, watching Monique through the dimly lit window. She had turned on the back-room lights, not the ones in front. Rosa felt her mother's hands on her shoulders. "Tap on the glass." Rosa was about to argue, but Mama pushed her forward, and she had little choice. She tapped lightly on the glass, her finger striking near the sign that still read, CLOSED.

Monique whirled around, then almost ran for the door and opened it, sticking her head out to look up the block, then down it. Her hair was in a perfect poodle, and Rosa was amazed to see that it had changed color again. Monique was now a flaming red-head. Last time she had been a Jean Harlow platinum blonde.

"Come in, come in," she said breathlessly. "And stay away from the windows. I don't want anyone to notice."

Rosa felt her mother's hands again, urging her forward. She took the first step, then hesitated. The smell of pomade and henna and old cigarette smoke blossomed from the open door, and it was almost more than she could stand.

"Come on!" Mama whispered.

Monique looked up and down the block again. "Hurry up, Rosie," she commanded, getting Rosa's name wrong as she always did. "I have about two hours to make you into a movie star and still end up with my job."

"Go," Mama said, gently pushing from behind.

"What's the matter, Rosie?" Monique asked. "Aren't you ready for a set of curls Miss Temple would die for?"

"Of course, she is," Mama said firmly, and she nudged Rosa inside the door.

CHAPTER SIX

Rosa's knees felt stiff. The beauty parlor looked unfamiliar and a little spooky with only the back room light on. Monique was hovering around, sliding past them and fussing over the permanent wave machine.

Rosa stared at it in the half-light. It looked like a nightmare monster with its dozens of cords snaking upward and connecting into the flat disk that stuck out from the upright stand. Rosa could not stop staring at it.

Come on, honey," Monique was saying. "We have to hurry a little here. This is going to take a couple of hours, and we open at nine o'clock."

Rosa nodded and tried to take her eyes off the contraption, but it was hard.

"Come on," Monique said, taking her hand. "You'll look beautiful. You'll love the curls." Still talking, she led Rosa all the way to the back of the shop and sat her in a sloping chair. "Sit down, stay put, and in two hours you won't know yourself, kiddo," she said, gently pushing Rosa into a reclining position.

Rosa felt the cool edge of the wash sink touch her neck. She had been shampooed and set in this very beauty parlor, twice—both times before auditions. And both times it had been oddly wonderful to have someone else fussing over her hair, washing and setting and combing it out. But she had never had a permanent wave done before.

"Relax, honey," Monique said. "You are stiff as a board." She laughed. "What do you feed her? Glue? Come on, honey, bend your knees, they're sticking out like fence pickets."

Rosa heard her mother laugh along with Monique, and she tried to relax. She closed her eyes and pretended that after the shampoo there would only be normal curlers or pin-curl rags—and then a gentle comb.

"There, honey," Monique murmured as her fingers went about their accustomed business, scrubbing Rosa's scalp and working thick lather through her hair. When the shampoo was rinsed out, Rosa opened her eyes in time to see a brown glass bottle in Monique's hands. "Close your eyes," Monique commanded. "In case I spatter a little."

Rosa closed her eyes and wrinkled her nose. Whatever the liquid was, Monique was saturating her hair with it. The odor burned her nose. Monique tugged her hair straight and coughed a little. No doubt the terrible fumes were bothering her, too. Rosa tried not to breathe in very deeply.

"One more little thing, and then we will get you in a chair," Monique said.

Rosa opened her eyes for a split second, trying to see what Monique was going to do next.

"Shut them tight!" Monique snapped.

Rosa squeezed her eyes shut instantly, blacking out the image of Monique hovering over her holding a dark cloth. Rosa could feel it being wrapped tightly around her head like a turban.

"Now, sit up, honey," Monique was saying. "And you can open your eyes again."

Rosa sat straight, the awful smell of the liquid stinging her nose. It made her eyes water, too.

"Into the chair," Monique commanded. She was smiling and turned to glance at Rosa's mother. "She will love it once we are finished."

Mama beamed. "I know she will, and so will those Paramount studio executives. They are going to take one look and Shirley will be in a breadline the next day, looking for work!"

Both women laughed. Rosa thought it was a mean joke, but she couldn't help but smile a little at the idea that she would be discovered—that she might be making movies.

"Over here," Monique said in a mock-stern voice. "Follow orders, soldier."

Rosa stepped forward hesitantly. Monique was motioning toward the chair set up directly in front of the permanent wave machine. She patted the seat. Rosa took a deep breath, then coughed on the fumes as she took three long steps and turned to sit down. The best thing to do was probably just get it over with.

"Now you keep real still, honey, and I can fly at this." Monique was already reaching for her wheeled side table, pulling it close. There were metallic rollers on it, and a stack of filmy squares of paper. Rosa glanced at her mother. She had found a copy of *Variety* and was reading it, leaning up against the back room door so the light fell on the page.

Rosa closed her eyes again. The fumes stung, but it was more than that. She felt odd, disconnected from herself. Monique's hands were moving fast again as she parted Rosa's thick hair into sections and wound it around the metal curlers, sliding the hinged covers in place, working the little papers beneath each one.

Monique stopped talking, and Rosa could hear her mother rustling the pages as she read about the top acts in the nation, on the vaudeville stage and on the silver screen. They had had to stop buying *Variety* again. Sometimes they could afford it, usually not. But it was always lying around in places like this, or at the trolley stops. They got their entertainment industry news a few days late, maybe, but they got it.

"Baby Peggy is still touring," Mama said aloud. "Imagine that. Washed up in the movies at seven years old, and then she just takes off on the road, and *voilà!* A hit. That girl is bursting with talent. And luck."

"They say her father was a real drill sergeant when she was just a tiny thing," Monique interjected. "Told everybody that it was his training that made her an actress—that she hadn't any more talent than the next kid."

"That's ridiculous," Mama exploded. "She sparkled on film, and everyone knows it. She's making a few pictures again now, someone said."

"She was nineteen months old in her first picture," Monique put in, shaking her head. "When was that, fifteen years ago?"

Mama nodded. "She started in silents when she was a year and a half, and she's sixteen now, or nearly. So it had to be about that," Mama said. "Think of that! Like Jackie Coogan. Those two struck it rich at an age when most toddlers are just learning to talk in sentences."

Rosa winced, listening to them talk. It was getting hard to ignore the fierce tugging and pulling on her hair as Monique wound the curlers into place. The stench of the liquid was as bad as it had been at first, but her nose had gone numb.

Rosa squeezed her eyes shut and wished they would stop stinging. If her hair curled, all this would have been worth it, she supposed. But what if it didn't? She let Monique's and her mother's words drift through her mind as she sat quietly, enduring the permanent wave.

Rosa had seen a lot of silent films, and she liked some of them. Others just seemed melodramatic and silly to her. Mama said Papa had thought the films with sound would never make it in the theaters. Lots of people had felt that way. They had all been proven wrong. Audiences loved the talkies.

Rosa loved musicals and dancing and the roaring sound effects of war and train crashes and the squeal of tires when the film showed a car rounding a corner. She loved trying to figure out how the spotlights had been placed in tricky shots, imagining what it would have looked like from a different angle. She liked everything about the movies, except having to audition.

"There," Monique said suddenly, and Rosa heard a clicking sound. "You'll feel them start to heat up now. You just tell me if it burns somewhere."

Rosa opened her eyes wide as the curlers started to get warm. Her mother and Monique were back to talking about the industry, but she couldn't make herself listen. The feeling of heat intensifying all over her scalp was too arresting. It was strange, as though she were standing in the hottest sun she could imagine, and incapable of moving into the shade.

The heat got worse and worse, until the curlers were hot enough to make her scalp start to tingle. She could feel her own pulse in her temples.

"Look!" Mama said, smiling at her. She held up a hand mirror. "That's not a sight you'd want a boyfriend to see anytime, is it? Lucky for you there are no photographers here just now."

Rosa gasped. Looking back at her from the little mirror was a flushed girl with electrical snakes spiraling upward from her scalp. The mirror was too small for her to see where they went, and it was all too easy to imagine them stringing all the way up through the ceiling. She tried to look up, but Monique gripped her shoulder. "You just sit still, honey. Don't pull anything loose or it could electrocute you."

Rosa glanced back at her, hoping it was a joke.

"Of course, I'm kidding." Monique laughed. "It's perfectly safe if you don't move."

"It'll all be over in an hour," Mama said, still smiling. "Then you'll see it was worth it. Right?"

"Right," Monique chimed in.

"Ouch," Rosa said. One of the curlers was burning its way into the nape of her neck.

"Where?" Monique asked, reaching for a little wad of the filmy paper.

Rosa pointed. "There."

Monique tucked the paper into place, and the worst of the burning stopped.

"How long do I have to stay like this?" Rosa asked, feeling a half dozen more hot spots starting on her scalp.

"Half an hour, usually," Monique told her. "But for hair as thick and straight as yours, probably forty minutes would be better." She glanced at her watch. "I'd better get them out in thirty-five. Wouldn't it be awful if Mrs. Bert picked this one day to come earlier than usual?"

"I would hate being the cause of any trouble for you," Mama responded instantly in an earnest voice that Rosa knew was a little fake. Not that she wanted to cause trouble for Monique, but she was making it sound like that was the worst thing she could possibly imagine, like something that would ruin her life forever. Mama was a very good actress. Rosa had no idea why she wouldn't audition for small parts at least.

Rosa listened for a few more minutes as Mama promised that she would pay Monique for the permanent as soon as they had the money. Rosa knew that much was true. Mama might fudge a little on things here and there, but she was honest about money and debts.

As they talked, Rosa tried to get her mind off the stinging heat that was increasing by the second as the electricity heated up the metal curlers.

"Let me make it this time," Rosa whispered a prayer as her mother and Monique began to laugh about something. She made her hands into fists and tried to pray so hard that the Virgin Mary would hear her and talk to God about granting her wish. "Let the studio men see that I am talented and determined and that I have worked hard and that Mama and Papa would be so proud of me," she added.

"What?" Monique said abruptly.

Rosa tried to shake her head, but the curlers and the weight of the electrical cords made it impossible. "Nothing," she said evenly. "Nothing at all." Rosa closed her eyes and waited for the time to pass. For a while she counted, but couldn't keep track of the chimpanzees and gave it up. She felt like she had been under the machine forever; she would never get out. Her scalp burned in tiny places, half-inch squares of terrible pain.

Rosa pointed at the worst places, and each time, Monique pulled the metal curler a tiny bit, then stuffed the soft paper beneath it. The relief from pain was so profound that Rosa sighed.

"She's all right," Mama said, hearing the long exhalation of breath.

No, I'm not, Rosa said inside her mind, where Mama wouldn't hear it and get angry with her for not being polite to Monique. And I hate it.

Taking out the curlers was even more painful than putting them in had been. Rosa didn't move an inch, fighting tears, as Monique sorted out the cords one by one, removing each curler slowly and carefully. When she was finished, Monique set a fan on Rosa, still talking cheerfully. "First one we did," she was saying, "we very nearly burned holes in that poor woman's scalp."

The heat was slowly dissipating in the fan's gentle breeze. Rosa realized she was gritting her teeth and relaxed her aching jaw.

"We've gotten much better at it," Monique added.

Rosa looked askance at her mother. She was pacing now, looking out the windows. The sun was coming up, Rosa realized, just bulging on the horizon like a ball of gold fire.

"Let me show you how to do this," Monique said, and Rosa watched her mother stop and turn to face the chair. Her face went entirely blank for a second, and then her eyes crinkled around the corners and she began to smile.

"Oh, sweeties, it looks perfect," she said, coming forward.

"Not yet it doesn't," Monique interrupted. "Come here. You need to learn how to do the comb-out properly."

Rosa sat rigidly as the two women fussed over her hair. She wanted to ask for a mirror, but she was afraid to. What was she going to look like with sausage curls hanging down beside her face?

"Mrs. Temple does it like so," Monique said reverently. "I saw her once on a set I was working on. They didn't let any of us touch that little Missy Temple, I can assure you of that. Her own mother always does her hair."

"Like this?" Mama asked, and Rosa felt a tentative tug at her hair.

"Yes, but pull it downward until it spirals out at the end."

"Like this?" Mama sounded unsure, and it made Rosa's stomach fluttery.

Monique patted her shoulder as though she had read her thoughts. "It looks gorgeous, like I promised, Miss Rosie. You just wait another minute or two."

Rosa sat as still as she could. The backs of her legs were aching from the hard chair seat, and her scalp was starting to itch like crazy.

"One more minute," Mama said. "I only have three more to do."

Rosa swung her legs back and forth, trying to ease the cramping pain. Then Mama reached around to tap her knee, and she stopped. She looked around the shop. The window was bright now, the early sunlight streaming in. The awful smell was less now, or maybe her nose had just gotten completely deadened by it and she couldn't smell anything anymore.

"Now you can look," Monique said. She handed Mama a mirror, half-bowing with a little flourish.

Mama bent forward and held it up, her face a mask of pure delight. Rosa moved a little to one side, leaning to fit her whole face in the image. Then she gasped. There, popping out all over her head and hanging down her neck, were big, fat sausage curls, almost exactly like Shirley Temple's except for the rich, dark color.

For a second, Rosa was too startled to say anything. Then, she smiled. "It's perfect," she managed. She looked into Monique's eyes. "Thank you so much. We can never repay you."

It sounded a little fake, like something her mother would say. She tried to think of something to add, but she couldn't, so she just stood there looking into the mirror.

Monique grinned. Then she laughed. "Yes, you can. And you'd better!"

"We will, we will," Mama promised. "Monique and I have that all worked out, sweeties." Then she laughed, too, thanking Monique as Rosa got up out of the chair. The long, spiraling curls bounced as she moved, and she stopped to reach up and touch them. They felt odd, stiff.

"Leave them be," Monique admonished her. "If you pull at them while the curl is still setting, they'll go straight."

Rosa lowered her hand instantly. She bent her knees and bounced up a little. The curls responded like springs, elongating, then coiling again on the rebound. It felt stranger than strange. Rosa giggled.

"I am happy to have been of help," Monique told her. "But now you two have to scoot. I have to get this place aired out and cleaned up before Mrs. Bert shows up."

"We really can't thank you enough," Mama said, guiding Rosa toward the door. Rosa murmured an agreement, and a second later they were standing outside the shop, blinking in the bright morning sunlight.

Rosa faced the beauty parlor windows and admired her image in its reflection of the morning sunlight. Then she heard a tapping sound and blinked. Monique was motioning them to get going, to get away from the shop. Rosa blushed and followed Mama up the sidewalk.

CHAPTER SEVEN

Walking back up Fountain Street, Rosa dawdled a little, just feeling the unfamiliar bouncing of her new curls. Mama walked fast as usual, and Rosa had to keep skipping a few steps to keep from falling behind. As they rounded a corner, Mama looked back over her shoulder. "We don't have to be at Paramount for hours," she said.

Rosa met her mother's gaze, still distracted by the entrancing bounce of her curls swinging out from her face, then brushing her cheeks. She reached up to touch her hair again. It felt odd and brittle. Mama reached out and gently pushed her hand down. "It looks perfect. Just leave it alone."

Rosa nodded, fighting the urge to touch her hair again. Why was it be so *stiff*?

"So, what do you want to do until show time? I don't have work today. Again," Mama added, looking disgusted. "I called last night, and no one needs me to wait tables today or tomorrow. And not a single tenant has plans to move, the manager told me. So I won't have cleaning for a while, either."

Rosa's stomach was churning. "I don't know, Mama. I'm nervous already."

"Nonsense," Mama interrupted. "You will knock them out of their chairs. It's going to happen this time, sweeties, I just know it."

Rosa nodded, and looked aside so that Mama wouldn't go into one of her long pep talks about how attitude and confidence made the whole difference. She was partly right, Rosa knew, but she was partly wrong, too. Every audition seemed to draw more girls. The last few had had huge turnouts, close to two hundred girls. How could anyone stand out in a crowd like that? It was hard to imagine anyone impressing the studio executives enough. It was like being in a parade.

At the last one, by the time her name was finally called—number 176—she had been numb and sick with nerves. But the studio men hadn't seemed to notice. In fact, on the hot soundstage they were using to audition girls, they had looked half-asleep. One of them had gone out just after she started, and had come back just as she finished, carrying a cup of coffee.

"Maybe we should go early, Mama," she said aloud. "Maybe the line will be first-come-first-served instead of alphabetical this time."

"It just depends on who is running it," Mama

said. "No way to know that until we get there."

Rosa shook her head, the foreign curls bouncing off her cheeks. "But if it's—"

"Alphabetical is better for us, sweeties. They don't like to pick too soon and they don't like to sit through the whole mob. 'M' is perfect. Moreno is the best name you could have on a day like today."

She said it in a funny voice, just being silly, but Rosa clung to her words. Moreno. Her father's name *was* a great name. He had been a great actor even if he hadn't been famous. Maybe some executive would remember his movies and wonder if she was his daughter. And maybe they would pay special attention to her audition. Maybe this time they would sit up straight in their chairs and she would see them realizing that she had it, that elusive quality that would make her a star. The sparkle Mama always said Rosa had enough of to light up a room.

"Rosa?" Mama interrupted her thoughts, stopping on the sidewalk.

Rosa looked up. "What?"

"What do you want to do? Go home and rest?"

Rosa shook her head. She hated the waiting more than anything else, and sitting in her room was the worst place of all. She had a sudden thought and smiled. "The library? Could we go this morning instead of—"

"Sweeties, we will go Wednesday, I promise you.

Cross my heart. But I don't think it's a good idea today."

Rosa felt her stomach tighten a notch. "Why not? It's cool and calm, and I love it and—"

"And you will have your head in a book instead of concentrating like you should on the audition," Mama finished for her.

Rosa looked away again. That was probably true, and that was exactly why she wanted to go. Reading would keep her mind off things, and she wouldn't get so nervous. She glanced at her mother and could tell by the expression on her face that there was no use arguing with her. At least she had promised, crossing her heart. Mama never broke promises when she crossed her heart.

"I know what," Mama said quietly. "We could go home and get something to eat, then go visit your father. Then we could just walk across the street for the audition."

Rosa nodded. Visiting her father's grave almost always made her feel better about everything. She had tried to explain that to Callie once, but Callie just thought she was crazy. It did sound weird, she knew. But it was true.

"I would like that, Mama," she said quietly, and shook her head gently just to feel the odd sensation of the curls swinging once more.

Mama smiled. "That's my girl. Let's go on home.

You really like your hair this way, don't you?"

Rosa nodded, because she could see how much her mother wanted her to say yes—but the truth was she wasn't sure yet.

"Okay then, sweeties," Mama said, swinging back around to start walking again. "Let's get this show on the road. *Vámonos.*"

Rosa laughed aloud and hurried to catch up. "Mama, your Spanish is awful."

Mama grinned. "You rattle it off perfectly to the Rodriguez kids, or when those old cowboys come around. I guess I thought you would forget how to do it eventually, without your father around to drill you at it like he used to do, but you haven't."

"Mama, it's Spanish," Rosa said evenly, surprised at how angry she felt all of a sudden. "It's a *language,* not some stage trick that I learned."

"Well," Mama answered, stepping off the curb to cross the street and talking over her shoulder, "I always told your father it was a good thing he could speak English, because I could never even try to learn that babble-jabber he spoke."

"Mama, you just said 'vámonos,'" Rosa snapped without meaning to. "That's Spanish, and you know exactly what it means. And you call me Rosita sometimes, and you shouldn't call it babble-jabber. That's an insult to Papa."

Mama stopped so suddenly that Rosa very nearly

ran into her as she spun around. They stood facing each other in the middle of the street. There wasn't much traffic this early, but Rosa glanced to see a dark sedan, stopped at the stop sign. The driver was a silhouette against the morning sun. It was a man, probably on his way to work.

"What did you say to me, young lady?" Mama demanded.

Rosa froze. She could feel her cheeks heating up. "I just said you shouldn't—"

"Rosita, you apologize right now for that tone of voice," Mama said sternly.

The car on the other side of the intersection honked. The driver made an impatient gesture, waving them out of his way. Mama stood her ground. She had a look on her face that Rosa knew meant there was no point in doing anything but apologizing.

"I'm sorry," Rosa said.

Mama's face softened. She hooked her arm through Rosa's and led her across the pavement. The instant they stepped onto the far curb, the man shoved the sedan into gear and roared across the intersection. Out of the corner of her eye, Rosa saw his angry face as he passed them.

"I loved your father," Mama said in a low, intense voice. "Every friend I had said it wouldn't work out because of all our differences, but it did and then we had you. Then we were twice as happy. Why do you think I haven't married again?"

Rosa stared into her mother's face. The idea of her remarrying had never even entered Rosa's mind. But now that Mama said it, Rosa was amazed at herself, assuming it would always just be the two of them. Mama was so pretty. She's probably had a lot of chances to go out. "Why?" Rosa asked timidly.

"Because your father was an impossible act for any other man to follow," Mama said without hesitation. "Oh, sweeties, maybe someday I will. I do get lonely. But you know how he was. He made us both feel so special and loved. And so safe."

Rosa nodded. It was true. Special, loved, and safe. She tried to think of how to say the same thing in Spanish, but couldn't seem to make Spanish words fit as exactly as the English ones did. Probably because they were Mama's words, Rosa thought. And they were perfect for once, like a well-written line in a movie—the kind that makes the audience cry.

"I think that we both have a case of nerves today," Mama said, breaking the silence that had settled over them. At that instant a second car passed, and Rosa turned to watch it speed by.

"Let's go home," Mama said. "I can press your costume while you make us some French toast. Or would you rather just have lunch early?"

"French toast would be good," Rosa said,

beginning to smile. "We still have that jar of honey Mrs. Rodriguez gave you last week."

Mama nodded. "Perfect, then."

Rosa waited, then when Mama started off, she followed, lengthening her steps to keep up. After a block or two, as they crossed another street, Mama reached out and Rosa took her hand and they walked on side by side.

CHAPTER EIGHT

By the time Rosa had the breakfast made, Mama had pressed her soldier costume and packed it in her costume box. They checked everything three times. Costume, tap shoes, extra shoe ribbons, the bright red bow for her hair. Their makeup bag was an old purse.

Mama had checked the things she always carried in her purse, too. She would have tissues and gum and the usual things, but that wasn't all. There was a package of hard candy in case Rosa's mouth got dry while they waited, and a cloth with resin dust in it for her hands so she wouldn't slip doing her cartwheels if her hands were sweaty with nervousness. Most important of all, there was her father's tiny mother-of-pearl cross. Rosa only wore it on special occasions, for luck.

Once they had gone through everything they would need to take to the audition, Mama sat down at the kitchen table and poured herself one more cup of coffee. Then she pulled a folded newspaper from her coat pocket. She rarely bought new papers, but she would pick up discarded ones in the restaurants she worked in or at the trolley stops if she found them clean and in good order. It embarrassed Rosa a little, but Mama said no one ever noticed.

"Two days old," she announced, flouncing the front page onto the table. "Do you think that will matter? If it's news to me," she added, repeating a joke she used often, "then it's news, right?"

Rosa hated reading newspapers. They all seemed to be one grim headline after another, about businesses failing and banks going under and desperate people looking for work. Sometimes the newspapers said good times were just around the corner, that everyone would be doing fine within a year. But it never came true.

"I think the movie business is about the only real depression-proof industry now," Mama said absently. "People find the money to go to the theaters, no matter what. In fact, the worse things get, the better the movies seem to do." Mama sighed. "Oh, listen to this, will you? Here's a man who thinks the hard times are going to go on another five or ten years." She read a paragraph of the article out loud.

Rosa murmured some response. She hoped not. It was awful already, with people not working, farmers losing their farms, factories closing down in the cities. It seemed to Rosa like she and Mama had been pinching pennies for as long as she could remember. But, of course, for them hard times had begun when her father had been killed six years before.

Mama kept her face buried in the newspaper, her legs crossed and her right shoe hanging loosely from her instep, her heel exposed. Her shoe swung back and forth, the only sign that Mama was anything but relaxed.

Rosa stood up and went back into her room for the fifth or sixth time. It was so hard not to stare in the mirror. It was like looking at a stranger. The curls bounced and swung, and she clasped her hands behind her back to keep from pulling on them. She had touched her hair three or four times when Mama wasn't looking, but she really didn't want to touch it again. It felt strange, rough and coarse, and she could tell that it wasn't as shiny as usual. And, worst of all, it smelled bad. Outside in the fresh air, she hadn't noticed, but now she could smell the stink of the liquid every time she turned her head. It smelled like wet diapers. Rosa turned on her heel and went back into the kitchen.

"Oh, you look so pretty," Mama said, looking at her over the top of the newspaper.

"Thank you, Mama," Rosa managed to say, but she felt uncertain about it now. In the mirror at the beauty parlor, she had looked pretty to herself. But now, she wasn't all that sure she liked having curls in her hair. And she *hated* the smell.

"You feeling all right?" Mama asked. "Your breakfast settling in okay?"

Rosa nodded. She did not want to talk about her nerves or her stomach or anything else that had to do with the audition.

"When do you want to go visit the cemetery?" Mama asked.

"We could go now," Rosa said, hoping Mama wouldn't think of some reason why they couldn't. She wanted to get out of the house, she wanted to get away from the mirror.

Mama nodded. "Fine with me. And let's go the long way around, all right? We can get a little soup or something at a luncheonette counter. We want to keep your strength up."

Rosa stood and went through her costume box one last time, then slid it beneath her arm. "I'm ready."

Mama laughed. "You are going to do fine today, Rosita. I just know it."

Rosa turned toward the door to avoid having to answer. If she said she would, Mama would tell her to concentrate, not to be overly confident. If she said she was nervous, Mama would tell her that was the kind of attitude that would dim her sparkle.

"Just let me brush my hair," Mama called out, going down the hall. "Not all of us have been to the beauty parlor this morning." She said it in a comically whining voice, as though she were the most pitiful, neglected creature in the world and Rosa could not help but laugh. When Mama came back, her hair perfect as always, they smiled at each other and went out the door.

Without saying anything more about it, they walked straight down Las Palmas, all the way to Hollywood Boulevard. Rosa was quiet, and was glad that Mama didn't seem to want to talk all that much, either.

The curls bounced with every step, so getting away from her mirror didn't help all that much. As she followed her mother across Fountain Street, Rosa looked down it, imagining herself walking toward the beauty parlor just hours before, her hair straight, shining, soft. The smell of the permanent wave was making her stomach queasy.

As they crossed to the center of the street to wait for the streetcar, Mama kept glancing at Rosa. They stood near the tracks, and Mama looked down the street. "Not coming yet," she said, then glanced at Rosa again. "It will take me a while to get used to the curls," Mama said when Rosa caught her eye.

Rosa nodded, wrinkling her nose. "Mama, I hate the way it stinks. Does the smell go away?" She crossed her fingers behind her back, hoping that the answer would be yes. Cars passed behind them and in front of them as the seconds ticked past.

Mama leaned forward and sniffed at Rosa's hair. She drew back so quickly that Rosa knew her hair smelled every bit as bad as she thought it did. "It does go away, though," Mama said quickly. "It does. A lot of my friends have had permanent waves, and they don't smell like that. Here, though . . . " She reached inside her purse and pulled out a little vial of perfume.

Rosa nodded eagerly. Mama dabbed a tiny speck of the perfume behind her ears and on her neck. "We don't want it too strong—" she began.

"It won't be," Rosa interrupted, not wanting her mother to say anything about the audition just yet.

"Here it comes. Get your nickel out," Mama said, putting away the perfume. Rosa heard the clanging bell and turned to see the streetcar approaching.

The car pulled to a stop, and the double doors in the middle opened up. Mama put her nickel in the coin box, and Rosa followed, dropping in her own fare. Two men came dashing across the street and hopped up the high steps just behind them. A woman waved and hurried to clamber up into the front door of the streetcar, waving her transfer paper at the conductor as she came.

Going down the narrow aisle, Rosa hoped the combination of perfume and wet-diaper smell wasn't going to make her even sicker than the bad smell had by itself. Mama hesitated, gesturing for her to take the window seat, and Rosa squeezed past her to sit down, her costume box on her lap. The window was open a little, and Rosa leaned her cheek against the glass for a second.

"You're all right, aren't you?" Mama asked in a concerned voice.

Rosa sat up straight again. "Yes, Mama. I'm fine." Then she turned to look out the window, watching the shops stream past. She liked to watch the women on Hollywood Boulevard. They were often dressed to the nines, on their way shopping. This morning, nearly every woman the streetcar passed had curly hair. Rosa wondered how many of them had permanent waves, and how many were blessed with hair like her mother's. She couldn't help but wonder how many of them smelled like wet diapers and perfume. She touched her scalp, just above her right ear. It stung as though she had burned it on the stove, and she pulled in a quick breath.

"What's wrong, sweeties?" Mama asked.

"It still hurts," Rosa whispered.

Mama looked startled, then narrowed her eyes. "It never really goes away, honey."

She looked so sad that Rosa knew instantly they had misunderstood each other, and she was too embarrassed to admit what she had really been saying—because she knew exactly what her mother had meant.

"I miss him every day," Mama said.

Rosa took her mother's hand, and they rode in silence the next few blocks. The prickly green fabric of the seat rubbed against the backs of her legs as the streetcar swayed to a stop at Wilcox Street. Two women, dressed nicely enough for a garden party, got on. They were chattering and laughing, and just looking at them made Rosa feel odd. They were blond, delicate-skinned women in their twenties, both beautiful.

"Aren't they lovely," Mama whispered.

Rosa nodded, watching the women seat themselves. They were. Mama nudged her. "Actresses, I think. This whole state is going to wind up beautiful, you know that? Because half of the ones who come will stay and have their families, and the pretty children will grow up and marry other pretty ones. It'll be like racehorses. They will get sleeker and better-looking."

Rosa looked aside as one of the women noticed her staring. "Stop it, Mama," she murmured. "Leave them alone."

Mama twisted back around. "They didn't notice me. They might have noticed you, pretty thing that you are. They probably took one look at you and now they are wondering if you are already a star." Mama was smiling.

Rosa frowned. "Stop it, Mama."

Her mother touched her arm. "I think maybe we both have a case of the nerves. This audition is such an important one for us."

The streetcar stopped at Cahuenga Street, and two elderly men got on, bickering over something. Rosa heard a few words clearly as they dropped their nickels in the box and went past to find seats. They were arguing over something President Roosevelt had said on the radio the night before. Rosa tried to understand what they were most upset about, the depressed bank rates or the labor unions starting up, but she couldn't.

"I am so sick of all the gloom and doom talk," Mama said after they had passed. Rosa nodded, then looked out the window again. As the streetcar started up she looked down the block to see the library. Mama noticed.

"We will go Thursday or Friday. I promise, cross my heart."

Rosa smiled. "Thanks, Mama." Just knowing that *something* was going to happen after today made her feel better.

"You feel all right?" Mama asked, searching her eyes.

Rosa nodded. "Fine."

Mama nodded back at her. "That's right. Just keep hold of yourself."

Rosa tried to smile and looked back out the window. At Vine, the streetcar stopped, and a family of tourists got on, their eyes big and round, staring at everything they passed. Rosa saw the mother looking at her, turning around to glance once more even after they had taken seats at the other end of the streetcar.

"They think you're a star, too," Mama teased.

Rosa started to protest, but then she saw the woman making a spiraling gesture with one finger, close to her own cheek. Rosa caught her breath. Were they saying something about her curls? Did the woman think the permanent wave looked silly? Rosa bit her lip, then resolutely turned her gaze back out the window until the streetcar stopped at Bronson Street.

Rosa tucked her costume box under one arm and reached toward the hatbox on the floor.

"I'll get it," Mama said, standing up, bracing herself with one hand as the streetcar came to a stop. Rosa stood, too, using one knee jammed against the seat in front of her to keep herself from falling until the streetcar braked.

Rosa followed her mother down the steep metal steps. As the streetcar clanged its way back into motion, they stood back, side by side, watching it go. Then Mama reached out and touched her curls. Startled, Rosa moved aside.

"I'm sorry," Mama said quietly. She looked hurt.

Rosa pulled in a deep breath. "I'm just nervous."

"We both are, sweeties," Mama said, using her baby talk voice. She put her arm around Rosa's shoulders and started her across the little raised streetcar platform. They crossed the street and then stopped on the sidewalk. The sun was high in the sky now, blazing down on Hollywood Boulevard. The white stucco buildings were bright enough to hurt Rosa's eyes.

"It'll take thirty minutes just to walk," Mama said, glancing at her watch. "It's hot. If I had the money, I'd call a cab." She smiled at Rosa, a forced, brittle smile. "Maybe we shouldn't have come the long way around."

Rosa shook her head. "I'm glad we did." Coming this way, they would come to the graveyard first, and she wouldn't have to walk past the arching gates of Paramount Studios until it was time to join the audition line.

"You feeling all right?" Mama asked again.

Rosa nodded. "I'm all right now."

Mama frowned, studying her face. "Are you sure?"

"I'm sure." Rosa started off, leading Mama down the sidewalk.

CHAPTER NINE

For a few blocks, they walked in silence. Rosa tried not to look at her reflection in the shop windows they passed, but it was hard. With every step, the bouncing curls tickled her neck in a way that her hair never had before.

"Do you want to get a soda or something?" Mama asked as they passed a little café.

Rosa shook her head. The idea of eating or drinking anything made her tight stomach feel even worse.

"Are you sure?"

Rosa tried to smile. "Yes, Mama."

Mama scrutinized her face again, and when Rosa tried to turn away, Mama caught her arm and pulled her back around. "Sweeties, this is a very important day for us, but I want you to relax a little if you can. You are going to do fine. Those studio men are going to sit up and realize they have a major new star on their hands. Believe me, they are going to just—"

"Mama?" Rosa cut her off, looking around

frantically for anything that would make Mama stop asking her how she felt, stop telling her about how the audition would go.

"What, Rosa?" Mama asked, her brow furrowing.

Rosa looked past her. "There," she said, pointing at a sign in a shop window. "They have beaded jackets on sale."

Mama frowned, turning. "Beaded . . . "

"Jackets." Rosa finished for her. She pointed again and Mama turned to look.

"We can't afford to buy anything, and I—" Mama began.

"But you could try on a few," Rosa interrupted. "You love window-shopping, and it'd be fun."

Mama took one step, then hesitated.

"We have plenty of time, and it'll keep our minds off the audition," Rosa said. "Come on, Mama," she insisted. "You always love trying on clothes."

Mama smiled. "You might be right, Rosita. Let's do." She hooked her arm through Rosa's, and they headed for the shop door.

It was cool inside. Rosa blinked, waiting for her eyes to adjust to the dimmer light. Mama let go of her arm and made a little sound of delight. "Oh, Rosa, just *look* at these," she breathed.

Rosa nodded politely at the woman standing in the back of the shop. The woman nodded back. "Is there anything I can help you ladies with?"

Mama tossed her hair. "Not just yet, thank you. We will call you when there is." She sounded like a queen telling her servants they should leave her alone for a while. Rosa blushed.

The woman frowned. Rosa knew she could tell that Mama wasn't going to buy anything. Rosa looked at Mama. Her dress was pretty, but it was cheaper-looking than anything in this shop. Rosa fingered the thin cotton of her own dress without meaning to. They really didn't belong in a store like this. But Mama was already lifting the hangers off the rack, squealing softly.

"Oh, Rosa, look."

Rosa turned and saw her mother hold up two beaded jackets, the hangers overlapping. One was velvet, the color of charcoal, with silver bugle beads sparkling across the lapels. The second one was lipstick red, shining silk, with glittering gold beading.

"Which one should I wear to your first premiere, sweeties?" she asked, loudly enough for the shop woman to hear her, smiling and tilting her head.

"Mama!" Rosa whispered. But her mother was already pulling on the first jacket, standing in front of the wall mirror. The dark velvet looked dramatic against her pale skin, and Rosa watched her turn sideways flattening the cloth against her body, smiling at herself in her reflection.

"Look at this!" Mama said, so quietly that Rosa

could barely hear her. Rosa nodded, an emphatic, exaggerated gesture that she hoped would keep Mama from saying anything else for the benefit of the shop woman.

"Rosa, isn't it just beautiful?" Mama whispered.

"Yes," Rosa said, meaning it. Her mother always looked beautiful in nice clothes. And Rosa was used to her trying things on without buying anything. But today, it was hard to pretend not to notice the irritated look on the clerk's face as Mama pulled off the smoke-colored jacket and pulled on the red one. "Oh!" she said aloud.

Rosa stared as the silk jacket transformed her mother into the kind of woman they saw at premieres when they stood outside with the rest of the crowd, hoping for a glimpse of a star.

"That's the one," Rosa said, her nerves subsiding as she looked at her pretty mother. The jacket was cut perfectly for her.

"Do you think so?" Mama asked, playing the game.

"Every conversation in the place will stop when you walk in," Rosa said.

Mama smiled. "Oh, now, sweeties . . . "

"It is gorgeous on you, Mama," Rosa insisted, and once again, she meant it. Her mother was a knockout, the kind of beauty every girl wanted to grow up to be.

Mama was pulling off the jacket. She put it back on the hanger, but then she laid both jackets over the rack instead of hanging them back up. Smiling, she pointed to the other side of the store. "They have a few things for girls your age," she said.

"Oh, no, Mama," Rosa said quickly, but her mother was already crossing the floor, her heels clicking on the red tiles.

"Rosa, oh, look at this one," Mama called out, pulling from the rack a light pink cotton dress with ruffles. "Try this one on, sweeties? It would look wonderful with your new curls."

Rosa shook her head, and the curls she didn't want to talk about touched her cheeks. Swallowing hard, she looked around, feeling as desperate as she had on the sidewalk outside. Her eyes fell on the jackets her mother had tried on, still draped across the rack. She glanced at the shop woman. She was frowning openly now, one hand on her hip.

"Rosa?" Mama's voice was a little sharper now.

Rosa snatched up the jackets, intending to hang them up properly, but the heavy, charcoal-colored velvet slithered free and fell to the floor. Rosa put the red jacket back on the rack, then bent to pick up the one that had fallen.

"Rosa, come on. You have to try something on," Mama called, and her voice was high and babyish. She was trying to be nice.

Rose straightened up, turning to face her. "I'll try this, Mama," she said on an impulse. And before her mother could say another word, she was sliding the charcoal velvet jacket on, her arm slipping through the heavy sleeve.

"Rosa?" Mama said just as she turned to look in the mirror.

Rosa frozel, staring at herself. The dark color of the jacket made her skin look luminous. The unfamiliar dark curls swung gently. She looked twenty, or at least sixteen. It took her breath away.

"Rosa! Take that off." Mama was standing beside her as though she had flown across the store. She was tugging at the velvet, pulling it free. She draped it over the rack and took Rosa's hand, yanking her back into the sunlight. Rosa had to lengthen her strides to keep up, but in her mind, she kept seeing the image of herself in the mirror. Mama always wanted her to look younger than she was for auditions. She always wore flounces and ribbons and cute ruffles. The girl in the mirror had been a complete stranger—a beautiful stranger.

When they got to the cemetery, Rosa heard Mama let out an exasperated breath. "I could have done without seeing *him* today."

Rosa looked down the graveled walk, past the trees. Pancho was standing beside her father's grave. His big sombrero was beneath his arm, and he was wearing chaps. His working costume. That meant he was probably on a picture at Paramount today. Rosa started forward.

"You go on ahead," Mama said tonelessly. "I'll wait here until he's gone."

Rosa hesitated, but just then Pancho looked up and saw them. There was a moment's pause, but then he waved. Rosa glanced at her mother.

"Go on, try to make it quick, please. I just can't stand to be around him today." She gestured to a bench beside the path. "I'll wait here. Leave the box."

Rosa handed Mama the costume box and watched her set it beside the hatbox on the bench. Then she sat down heavily, making a shooing gesture with one hand. "Go on, Rosa, we don't have too much extra time, and I am starting to get nervous again, are you?"

Rosa nodded, but the truth was, for the first time all day, she felt almost calm. Smiling her thanks at her mother, she started forward. Pancho watched her come, stepping back from the grave.

"*¿Cómo está, mi niña?*" he asked when she got closer.

She smiled. Pancho always asked her how she was. His big, dark eyes were steady and calm on hers. "*Bien, bueno,*" she told him, trying to smile brightly. But then the truth slipped out. "*Tengo preocupes esta día.*"

"The audition?" he asked, switching to English. "Is that what you are worried about?"

Rosa nodded. He patted her head. "Nerves are part of the job. but you will do well, rosa. I am sure of it." He looked at the grave again. "I came to tell your father good-bye. I am leaving in a few days."

"Leaving?" Rosa echoed.

"Yes," Pancho told her. "The movies have finally paid for my *rancho* and my cattle. It is time I went home to help my sons."

"Home." Rosa said the word as though it were in a language she didn't speak. It never had occurred to her that Pancho had another home.

"Hermosillo," he said. "Where your father and I were boys."

"Papa grew up in Texas," Rosa corrected him.

"No, Rosa. He went there at sixteen, then came to Hollywood at twenty."

Rosa didn't know what to say. Her father never had talked about Mexico. Or maybe he had and she had just been too little to understand.

"Your father wrote me and told me to come here, too," Pancho said. "He knew my ambition to own land, to raise cattle—it was his dream, too."

Rosa could only stare. Then she licked her lips and looked at her mother, sitting with her back straight and her head high. "He wanted to be a star, too, though," she said quietly. "More than anything."

Pancho shook his head. "Your father loved to ride a good horse under the open sky. If he had lived, he would have had his own *rancho* long before this. I have been slow because I send money to my sister. Her husband cannot work." Pancho pressed a hand to his back and grimaced, pantomiming his brother-in-law's pain.

Rosa blinked and glanced back toward her mother. Mama waved, an impatient little gesture. Pancho hesitated, then waved at her. She turned slightly, staring back out toward the street without responding.

"I will come see you tomorrow or the next day, to say a real good-bye, Rosa," he said, putting his hat back on his head. The intricate embroidery shone like colored spiderwebs in the sun. He stroked his mustache. *"Buena suerte,"* he said, wishing her good luck the way her father had always done.

"Thank you, Pancho."

He smiled. "Rosita?"

She looked at him, waiting for the question.

"What have you done to your hair?"

Rosa blushed. "It's called a permanent wave. Does it look awful?"

Pancho shook his head. "No. But, it is permanent? *Parasiempre?"*

Rosa smiled and shook her head, and felt the curls bounce. "No, it'll grow out."

Pancho looked relieved. "It will be straight and shiny again?"

"Yes," Rosa told him. "And the smell goes away."

Pancho's smile broadened. "That's good." He grinned, and Rosa grinned back. "Dance like your Papa would want you to dance," he said.

Rosa nodded. "Mama says that, too," she told him.

He arched his heavy eyebrows and stroked his mustache again. "But I think we don't mean exactly the same thing," he said after a long pause. "Your father is very proud of you."

"I miss him, Pancho."

He patted her head again. *"Tambien yo,"* he said sadly. "So do I."

Rosa watched him walk away, his hat pulled down tight, his long stride covering the ground fast as he headed for the Paramount lot. Once he was out of sight, she heard her mother.

"Rosa?"

Rosa turned. Mama was coming up the path. "That took long enough. What was he saying?"

"Did you know that Hermosillo is in Mexico, Mama?" Rosa asked.

Mama's face darkened. "Of course. Why?"

"I thought it was in Texas, like Amarillo. I never knew Papa grew up in Mexico."

"He didn't, really," Mama said. "I mean, he became a citizen years before I met him. What difference does it make?"

Rosa didn't answer. She walked to her father's grave and sat down beside the headstone as she usually did. Mama sighed loudly and came to join her "I want you to tell me the truth about Papa," Rosa said, staring up at the trees..

CHAPTER TEN

The audition line was long, even though they got there an hour before first call. They saw the end of it as they walked through the wrought-iron gates, following the steady parade of cars that turned into the entrance.

"Have we ever seen an audition line this long this early, Mama?" Rosa asked in a whisper as they took their place in line behind fifty or more women and their daughters.

Mama shook her head. "I think there's some mistake. Or there are two or three parts being cast and they have just put everyone all together."

Rosa shifted her feet on the crushed gravel. The soles of her shoes were worn pretty thin. The line went around the corner of the building in front of them. They couldn't see the head of it from where they stood. "We should at least walk up and check the sign, shouldn't we?"

Mama nodded. "We should. Do you want to go, or stay here and hold our place?"

Rosa shifted her weight again. Waiting was the hardest part. "I'll go."

"But come straight back. Don't stop to talk to anyone."

Rosa nodded automatically, without really hearing what her mother had said. She handed Mama the costume box and stepped out of line.

"Come right back," Mama said again.

Rosa nodded, then started walking. The line was fairly orderly back where Mama remained standing, but as Rosa went forward, it widened so that three or four girls—and their mothers—stood abreast.

"First come," one mother said as Rosa made her way past. Rose glanced at her. The woman was smoking, holding the cigarette between her lips, grimacing to keep the smoke out of her eyes. Her daughter was blond, Rosa saw, with pin curls framing her face like an actress from the twenties. For the first time Rosa noticed that a few of the girls were already wearing their costumes.

"I was just walking to the front to ask some questions," Rosa told the woman. "Isn't there a changing room?"

The woman blew smoke straight up, then lowered her chin again. "I don't know. The first one we went to that didn't have a changing area was so bad that we just come dressed now."

Rosa looked at the woman's daughter. She

looked very young—perhaps four or five. "Isn't this role a little old for her?" Rosa asked in a polite voice.

"If I thought that I wouldn't be here, would I?" the woman snapped. She turned aside and bent to say something into her daughter's ear.

"I'm sorry," Rosa mumbled, and started forward again.

The line disintegrated into an unraveled knot of people standing near the front. They were packed in shoulder to shoulder, the mothers edging a few inches at a time toward the front.

"Excuse me," Rosa said, turning sideways to fit between two women. One of them moved slightly to let her through, but a tall brunette with her hair pulled back from her face in a severe style scowled at her.

"First come," the woman said.

Rosa nodded. "I know, ma'am. I just want to get close enough to read the signs or to see if there's anyone to answer questions." The woman exhaled sharply, but didn't say anything more as Rosa slid past.

At the front of the line there was a man leaning against the studio wall. In the sea of women and girls, he stood out like a sore thumb. Rosa made her way toward him, murmuring "excuse me" every few seconds. Some of the women waited until she tapped them on the shoulder, but then, one by one, they moved aside.

"Sir?" Rosa said when she was close enough.

The man seemed not to hear her.

"Sir?"

He turned and looked past her. Then his eyes drifted across her face, and she addressed him once more. He focused on her. "Yeah?"

"Is this the audition for the girl's personality lead?"

The man nodded, then took out a toothpick and set it in the corner of his mouth. "Yes, it is."

Rosa tried to keep his eyes from straying away by smiling at him, but it didn't work. "Sir? " she said a little louder. "Is it alphabetical or—"

"With this many?" he interrupted her. "Are you nuts?"

"Is there a dressing room?"

The man shifted his toothpick from one corner of his mouth to the other. "Yeah. They'll bring you in three or four at a time, everybody gets changed, then they'll run you through while the next batch changes."

Rosa thanked him and started back through the crowd. It was easier going back. No one cared or even noticed that she was walking past. She looked into the faces of the girls as she went. Some were laughing and chatting, but most of them were silent and nervous-looking. A few looked pale and sick, and Rosa tried to smile at them. Poor little girls—some of them looked like they were barely five.

"There's no order," she told Mama when she got back.

"Did anyone compliment your curls?" Mama asked.

Rosa shook her head. "Mama, they are all nervous and they all thought I was butting in line."

"Maybe we should try to move up," Mama said. "Oh, I knew we should have gotten here sooner. We never should have stopped at the cemetery. And it just upset you, I can tell."

Rosa shook her head. For some weird reason, her stomach was calmer than usual. "I'm all right."

Mama looked at her. "Your hair looks pretty. We'll brush it the way Monique showed me just before you go on."

Rosa nodded. "With a line this long, it could be hours."

Mama made a little sound of dismay. "I hate the waiting."

Rosa met her eyes. "So do I. And it's hot."

Mama touched her forehead. "Do you think you have a fever, or is it just nerves, sweeties?"

Rosa took a step back, trying to smile. "I only meant it's a hot day, Mama. I'm all right."

"Changing room?" Mama asked.

Rosa nodded. "Groups of three or four."

Mama frowned. "Maybe that means they are going to run girls through fast, or even in pairs. Remember that one on the Fox lot, where they made you dance to music you had never even heard with three other girls?"

Rosa nodded. Actually, now that she remembered it, she had kind of enjoyed it, because all she could do was tap freestyle instead of being terrified about forgetting part of her routine.

"How long ago was that?" Mama asked.

Rosa tried to remember. "A year ago. No, more like two years, because I remember leaving Mrs. Higgins's class to go that day."

"Two years," Mama said dreamily. "And we've been auditioning for nearly seven. We have been to our share of these, haven't we?"

Rosa shrugged. "It seems like we have been to thousands."

"Well, today is our lucky day," Mama said, and her face set in a determined expression. "Today will be it. One of those studio men is going to—"

"We'll just have to wait and see how it goes," Rosa interrupted.

Mama looked hurt. "I am just trying to keep your spirits up and be a good mother."

Rosa shifted her weight. "Look, Mama." She pointed. The line behind them was growing fast. There were trickles of girls and mothers coming in from the gate and the parking lots. They joined together to add to the main line, then stood, talking among themselves, or standing quietly.

"Well, then. Nothing to do but wait," Mama said. She was silent a full minute, looking around, then she focused on Rosa again. "How are you feeling? I am so nervous, I could explode."

Rosa looked at her mother, wondering how many times she usually asked that question. Rosa never had thought about it before—because she had always been so nervous. All her life she had thought that her face was pale or that her nerves showed in some way that made Mama ask. But today she was almost calm for a change, and Mama asked, anyway.

"Feeling all right?" Mama repeated the question. Rosa nodded. "Better than usual."

"Not me," Mama said slowly, touching her forehead. "I am really sweating this one out, and it isn't just the sun."

Rosa looked at her, wondering something else for the first time. "Why, Mama?" she said aloud. "You don't have to dance or anything." Rosa watched her mother's face collapse into an expression of hurt and confusion and was sorry she had said anything at all.

"I just mean you aren't the one who has to—" she began, but Mama cut her off.

"What are you saying, Rosa? That I have no right to be nervous?"

Rosa swallowed hard, staring at her mother. "I only meant you don't have to be. That I am the one—"

"Have you forgotten the hours I spent making

that costume? All the costumes? Have you forgotten the lessons I have paid for? And singing coaches and sheet music and your elocution teacher and . . . everything!" Mama's voice was pitched low, but it still had an edge to it.

Rosa noticed two of the mothers looking at Mama, their faces clearly disapproving. They were probably worried that an argument would upset their own daughters. Mama noticed them, too, and mumbled an apology. Then she leaned close. "It's just a very strange thing for you to say, Rosa."

Rosa shrugged awkwardly and tried to smile. "I was just trying to make you feel better, Mama."

"It made me feel just the opposite of better," Mama hissed beneath her breath. Rosa was amazed to see tears in her mother's eyes.

"I'm sorry, Mama."

"I know you are the one who has to dance," Mama said in a low voice.

Rosa had no idea what to say, so she just took her mother's hand and held it without speaking. Silence thickened between them. They were a little island of quiet in the line, surrounded by voices.

The sun rose higher in the sky before the line finally inched forward. The auditions were starting. Rosa felt her stomach tighten a little, but not as much as usual. She felt like she was in a dream this time, like the audition wasn't quite real or as important as she had thought. maybe what Pancho had said had helped. She would dance as her father would have wanted—Papa, whose dream had been cattle and a ranch, not stardom.

A murmur went through the crowd, all the girls shifting on their feet, standing straighter. "They're starting," someone in front of them called out.

A sigh went through the line, and Mama squeezed Rosa's hand, then released it. "Well, here we go, then. It won't be too much longer." She glanced behind them. "I pity those poor souls in the back. They could be here until nightfall—unless they send everyone home after they see you."

"Please don't, Mama," Rosa begged.

"Don't what?" Mama said, and her eyes looked glossy again.

Rosa bit her lip, keeping her mouth shut. The line moved forward again.

"Are they moving them through that fast?" Mama wondered aloud.

Rosa shrugged. There was no way to know, of course, but Mama always asked questions like that while they were waiting, to pass the time. Just then, Mama leaned forward and tapped the mother standing in front of them. "Excuse me?"

The woman turned around. "Yes?"

Mama smiled tremulously. "I just wondered, if they are in the same group, perhaps your daughter would like to meet mine before they go in?"

The woman nodded politely and reached down to turn her little girl around. And she *was* little. She looked about six. "Charlotte," the woman said, bending down so that her daughter would hear her over the shuffling and talking around them. "Charlotte this is . . . ?" The woman looked up.

"Rosa," Mama said loudly and proudly. Rosa bent her knees so that she could look into Charlotte's face. "I'm Rosa."

Charlotte made a face. "Do we have to dance?"

Rosa nodded. "It's an audition."

Charlotte made another face. Rosa could hear their mothers talking over their heads, exchanging complaints about standing in the sun.

"I feel sick," Charlotte said.

Rosa nodded. "I have before. A lot of girls do."

"Then why are we doing this?" Charlotte said. "My mother says I have to, but I hate it. And they never pick me, anyway."

"Maybe today they will," Rosa said kindly.

Charlotte went pale. "I hope not. Mother says it's like one long, glorious recital. But I *hate* recitals."

Rosa smiled and wished there were something she could say to help poor Charlotte. She looked like a starving waif in some epic saga, her eyes huge with fear and her skin sheet-white. She would be perfect in that kind of part. "It's okay," Rosa said aloud. "Even if you do get picked, you'll probably just be an extra or something. That's fun."

"It is?"

Rosa nodded. "Like a group number at a recital. It's easy. And they pay you ten or fifteen dollars a week—or more, sometimes."

Charlotte's eyes went wide. She glanced up at her mother, then at Rosa again. "I'd like that."

Rosa nodded and whispered close to her ear, "So would I."

"Rosa?" Mama said from above her.

"Is being an extra really fun?" Charlotte asked.

"Yes," Rosa told her, ignoring her mother. "The sets and the cameras are really interesting, and the actors are usually pretty nice." Charlotte looked so relieved that Rosa smiled.

"Thank you, Miss Rosa," Charlotte said politely, curtsying like in dance class.

Rosa straightened up. Mama was staring at her. "What were you two talking about for so long?"

Rosa shrugged. "She's so nervous, she feels sick. I told her not to worry."

Mama leaned close. "I hope you didn't make her relax enough to sparkle too bright. The little ones are the ones you have to worry about the most at your age, Rosa."

Rosa blinked, unsure of what to say.

"Look at the one in front of her," Mama said

close to her ear. "She's awfully cute with that wispy brown hair. But I bet she can't dance. She's pigeon-toed."

Rosa turned to look at her mother. Had she always been like this? Had they always spent their time waiting in lines gossiping and hoping no one else did very well? Rosa pulled in a long breath, trying to recall. For her, the long audition lines had mostly been a torture as she fought her nausea and tried not to let her stomach tighten enough to choke off her breath, making her vomit.

"All the ones I can see are small," Mama said, craning to look forward, then back. "That doesn't mean there aren't older girls farther back."

Mama reached out and took Rosa's hand and squeezed it tightly, holding on. "How are you feeling?"

"I'm all right," Rosa told her, and faced forward as the line moved up another notch.

"I'm a little better, too," Mama answered, smiling a nervous smile.

Up the line Rosa could hear a man's voice calling out something she couldn't quite understand, but she knew it must be the next group being called in. She wanted to ask her mother if she remembered her promise about the library, but knew it would irritate her. Rosa pressed her lips together to keep from saying anything.

"Just concentrate on the routine," Mama said.

"That's all you should be thinking about now."

Rosa nodded. As Mama squeezed her hand and fell silent, though, she found herself thinking about everything but her routine. She felt sorry for poor little Charlotte. She felt sorry for the people in the back of the line who would probably be here the whole day, waiting. Glancing up at the fiercely sunny sky, she saw a seagull flying fast and low, and she wondered where it was going.

"Just keep going through the routine in your mind," Mama said. "Then when you get in there, it will come automatically. Remember, you'll have the new arrangement. Don't let that throw you off, sweeties."

"I won't, Mama," Rosa said, still watching the seagull as it disappeared into the clear blue of the sky.

CHAPTER ELEVEN

"Next group, and please, ladies, don't push!" the man was shouting. Rosa stepped forward as Charlotte and her mother did and followed them. Rosa breathed in the stale smoke odor of the building. She hoped the studio executives would not be smoking cigars. Sometimes they did, and the smell made her stomach even queasier than usual. Maybe it would just be the director doing the casting, or just the director and one or two of the stars. If they were big enough names, they had some say in who would be chosen to play opposite them.

Rosa wondered who was starring in the film she was auditioning for. The announcement hadn't had any names in it, just a description of the part.

"This is it!" Mama was saying from beside her.

Rosa's stomach was tighter now, and she welcomed the nervousness in a way. It was familiar. She suddenly thought of the Spanish word *familia*—family. She whispered them both as she walked into the studio building. Familiar, *familia*—family. Her stomach loosened a little.

"Just keep dancing it in your mind," Mama said from behind her. "I read that's what Shirley Temple was taught to do, sweeties. So just keep—"

"Mama, please." Rosa looked at her mother. "I won't forget the routine."

"This way! In here, please!" a man's voice shouted close by. Rosa looked up. He was directing them down a narrow hall. The walls were painted gray, and there were scuff marks and stains along the floorboards. Little Charlotte was crying quietly. The girl in front of her was chattering like a sparrow. Mama was right, she was pretty. Her light brown hair fell in wispy waves down her back. Rosa stared at the girl's legs as she walked stiffly forward. Mama was right about her being a little pigeon-toed, too. But she was so cute, it was charming on her.

"This way, ladies," another voice boomed out. "Mothers and daughters for the audition, this way!"

They filed through another door, and Rosa found herself wondering if Pancho was still working on the far side of the lot where most of the Western films were made. He probably was. Or maybe he only had a shot or two left in the film and he had gone home by now.

"Let's go, girls."

Rosa looked up. She could see the dressing room matron now, a big woman with a gravelly voice. She was ushering in the wispy-haired girl, then Charlotte and her mother. Then it was Rosa's and Mama's turn. Behind them came another pair.

"Four at a time, please," the matron said, closing the door solidly in the faces of the next pair in line. "There are tables over there," the woman said, pointing. "And we've only got one mirror, so please take turns."

"That's fine," Mama said. "It's nice to have a place to change." Rosa smiled at the woman, too. She took no notice, going right on to recite the information a second time to someone else. Rosa glanced back. The fourth girl had bright red hair and freckles. She had striking blue eyes, and skin so pale that it looked translucent.

Rosa faced front again and walked behind her mother into the room. It *was* nice to have a private place to dress. A lot of auditions didn't provide anything more than a blanket hung up across a storeroom door, especially at the smaller studios, where money was tighter and the soundstages were surrounded by muddy alleyways. They changed in hallways sometimes, or broom closets.

As Mama led the way, Rosa tried, for the first time, to run through her routine in her mind. Still concentrating, she followed Mama to one of the little tables and set down the costume box. She stood very still, imagining her routine in her mind.

"Smile, sweeties," Mama said just as she finished.

Rosa looked up, distracted from her thoughts.

"Smile, Rosita," Mama said, grinning as though Rosa would not understand the words and needed an example.

"I will, Mama," Rosa said. "Once I am in there." She glanced around. "Mama, could you get the costume out? I need a bathroom."

"Just ask the matron, Rosa," Mama said. "But hurry back. They won't wait for you. Are you sick?"

Rosa shook her head. "I just need to use a bathroom."

Mama's smile thinned into a nervous grimace. "Just hurry, Rosa. Shoo. I'll get everything laid out for you to hop straight into when you come back."

Rosa nodded and started off, her stomach winding up one more notch. Mama looked pale. All the mothers looked tense, she saw, walking across the room. And their daughters looked even worse. Rosa turned to look at her mother and found Mama staring after her, a tentative smile on her face. Rosa smiled back, and Mama waved, as though the twenty or so feet that separated them was a journey in itself.

"But you'd better be back before you're called," the matron said, when Rosa asked her about the bathroom. Then she pointed. "Around the corner to your right, then up the hall—it's on the left side."

Rosa waved once more at her worried-looking mother, then hurried out. She met the next group of mothers and daughters standing in the hallway.

"Are there stars?" one of the girls asked eagerly as she passed. She had curly blond hair that appeared dull and stiff like Rosa's. Rosa wondered if hers still smelled bad.

Rosa shrugged. "I haven't been inside to audition yet. I just needed a bathroom."

"Where is it?" the girl asked. "Mommy, can I go, too?"

"If you hurry," the woman told her daughter. "Just run quick and get back here."

"Excuse me, I have to hurry, too," Rosa said, nodding politely at the group and walking on her way. But the younger girl ran to catch up with her.

"My name is Laura. What's yours?"

Rosa introduced herself without slowing down. When they got close to the bathroom door, she slowed and caught Laura's eye. "Permanent wave?"

Laura looked around suspiciously, then nodded. "Mama said not to tell anyone."

"Does the smell go away?"

Laura nodded. "Finally. It takes weeks."

Rosa sighed and pushed open the door. A woman coming out very nearly ran into her. She was dark-haired and beautiful, and she was wearing a teal silk blouse with velvet trousers the color of dark mink.

"Excuse me, please," Rosa managed. "I'm very sorry."

The woman only smiled. "I should look where I am going, too. Don't apologize."

Rosa swallowed hard. "Are you a star?"

The woman shook her head. "Not me. I don't like being in front of the cameras all that much."

Rosa stared at her. "I love being an extra, too. Then I get to see it all, the cameras and lights and everything, but I don't have to worry so much."

The woman laughed, a high, quick, wonderful laugh that arched her back and lifted her chin toward the ceiling. Then she reached out and touched Rosa's cheek. "May you reach your dreams, dear. Half the trick is knowing what you want."

Rosa watched the woman walk away, transfixed. How could someone that beautiful *not* be a star?

"Are you going in?" Laura asked.

"You go first," Rosa told her, not wanting to turn away until the beautiful woman was out of sight.

Laura went into the bathroom. A few seconds later, Rosa heard the sounds of someone throwing up. It made her stomach writhe, but she managed not to get sick herself. When Laura came out she looked pale and sweaty, but she was smiling. "Mama always makes me eat before we come, and I almost always have to do this. I just don't tell her anymore. She gets so upset."

Rosa nodded vaguely, forcing herself to go into

the smelly bathroom. She hurried and was back out two minutes later. Laura hadn't waited for her. Nearly running, Rosa started back. When she passed Laura she wished her luck, and Laura wished her well, too. Laura's mother just stared without speaking.

Back in the dressing room, Rosa saw her mother's face light up as she walked in. "I was so afraid you'd get mixed up or something," Mama breathed. "That you wouldn't make it."

Rosa let her mother nudge her toward their part of the dressing table. Rosa peeled off her dress as Mama opened her costume box. The shining black satin trousers slid on like water, cool and welcome. The bright red jacket fit her perfectly, Mama always saw to that. As Mama buttoned the frogged gold braid loops over the brass buttons, her hands were trembling. She patted on the round circles of bright rouge and put lipstick on Rosa's lips. Then she painted the soldier's black, curled mustache on Rosa's upper lip. It tickled, but Rosa had learned not to move a muscle so that Mama could get it perfect.

Rosa settled her tall soldier's cap on her head, positioning the strap along the front of her chin. The strap was cloth, so it was soft, but Mama had sewn black bangles all over it, so from a distance it shone like polished leather—just like a toy soldier's would have. Mama fastened Papa's cross around Rosa's neck, then tucked it inside her jacket. Her hands were ice-cold.

Rosa wanted to say something to make her feel better, but the truth was she was getting pretty nervous herself. It felt different from her usual nervousness though. Usually by the time their call was this close, she was fighting not to be sick. This time, she just felt fluttery.

"Next, please," a woman said, banging open a door on the far side of the room.

Rosa jumped involuntarily, and Mama gasped, startled. Little Charlotte cried louder. The woman looked bothered and impatient. "Who's ready here?"

"I am," Rosa said without thinking.

"We are, too," the mother of the red-haired girl called out from their table nearest the door.

"You first," the woman said, pointing at her. "You second." She gestured at Rosa. "You third," she said, jabbing a finger in the direction of the girl with the wispy hair. "You last," she said to Charlotte. "And stop crying, because we can't wait on you, not even a minute. Too many to see today." She looked at a clipboard in her hand, lifting the top sheet. "Names?" she asked the ceiling, then looked down at the wispy-haired girl. "Name?"

"Theresa Bradley," the girl's mother answered.

"Rosa Moreno," Mama said.

"Charlotte Zeiler," Charlotte's mother said very clearly. And then she spelled her daughter's last name over the sound of her daughter crying.

The red-haired girl's mother stood tall, hesitating until the woman looked up at her. "This is Miss Gladys Burnstock." She said it so loudly and so clearly that she sounded like an announcer on the radio. Her daughter curtsied, her green tutu flaring up behind her. She had on tap shoes that looked like ballet slippers, Rosa saw. And her hair was dotted with tiny green bows.

The woman at the door only frowned a little deeper. "All right," she said, "let's go. Don't make them wait." She spun around, and the door slammed behind her.

CHAPTER TWELVE

There was a breathless pause as the red-haired girl and her mother crossed the room. Rosa smoothed the red side-stripe on her black silk trousers as they headed out the door.

"Mother?" The woman nearly shouted as they walked past her. "Mother! You stay back here with me." The woman was frowning as the door closed again.

Rosa caught a glimpse of the stage, a nice, wide one, and of folding chairs set up just in front of it. There were spotlights on, she saw, then the door closed.

Mama sighed, and Rosa looked at her. "Don't let the arrangement throw you," Mama said. "Maybe we shouldn't have done that. Maybe we should have stayed with the one you know so well and—"

"It won't bother me, Mama," Rosa said, just wanting her to be quiet again.

Mama pushed her hair back off her face and

sighed again. "Have you gone all the way through it mentally?"

"Yes." Rosa avoided her mother's eyes. It was true, she had, but only once. "I'm going to stretch a little, Mama," Rosa said, hoping there wouldn't be any more questions.

There was no barre, but the edge of the table worked well enough. Rosa started slowly, the way she had been taught, leaning her torso smoothly, one arm arced high over her head. She changed legs.

The sound of a piano came suddenly through the wall where the door stood closed. The whole room went quiet as the thumping counter-bass of a ragtime number began. Good choice, Rosa thought. Old-fashioned, but everyone still likes ragtime music. And it was different. Most of the girls chose movie songs or the orchestrations from production numbers in last year's films. Sometimes they even tried to replicate the routines of famous child stars. Mama had always said that was silly. Why would a studio want to discover someone just like someone else they already had under contract?

The ragtime rose to a pitch and thudded along at crescendo-ferocity. Rosa could hear the clicking of the red-haired girl's taps. Gladys, she corrected herself. Gladys's taps.

"How are you feeling?" Mama asked.

Rosa took a deep breath, wishing her poor

stomach didn't have to clamp down so hard every time she auditioned. "I'm all right," she said to her mother.

The piano suddenly fell silent, and Rosa found herself turning to stare at the door with everyone else. You could usually tell how someone had done, just by the expression on her face.

The door banged open, and Gladys came through it, her mother close behind. Their eyes were downcast, their expressions grim.

"Now if you sparkle, you'll really stand out," Mama whispered.

Rosa frowned, wondering again if Mama had always been so unkind, or if she had just been to too many auditions with a daughter who was never the one chosen for the lead. Rosa hoped she could at least get a little part, or some extra work on this movie. They needed the money with Mama not working steady lately. She wondered if she had to ask the director to be considered for extra work.

"Next!" the woman at the door called out. Mama turned and stared, her usual grace turned suddenly stiff.

Rosa stretched once more, quickly, then started for the door behind her mother. The woman called Mama back as she had the woman before her, and Rosa walked forward onto the stage by herself.

"But I have the sheet music," Rosa heard her mother saying. There was some low reply from the woman. Then, Mama called out, "Rosa, here. They want you to carry it to the pianist."

Rosa stopped and turned back, daring a glimpse at the chairs below the edge of the stage for the first time. She very nearly stumbled and fell.

The woman she had bumped into outside the bathroom was sitting in the center chair nearest the stage. There were two other people seated a little behind her. Rosa felt herself blush. Of course the woman was a star. She had *looked* like a star. She just hadn't wanted to sign autographs in the hallway.

Rosa looked at her mother, then, without stopping, she glanced again. There were two men in the side chairs. One of them looked like Douglas Fairbanks, Jr.

"Here," Mama whispered, thrusting the sheet music at Rosa. She took a breath to say something else, but the studio woman held up her hand. "Just let your daughter audition, please, ma'am. We don't have much time."

Rosa meant to smile at her mother as she turned back, but she ended up staring at the woman again, then glancing at the chairs behind her. Rosa caught her breath. It *was* Douglas Fairbanks, Jr., she was pretty sure. Mary Pickford's handsome stepson. It was too dark in the house to be sure—all the lights were dimmed, and the stage spots were bright—but it looked like him. So the other man had to be the director.

Rosa handed the pianist the music and gave her a polite curtsy. The woman smiled. "Do you like it up-tempo?" Her voice was businesslike but warm. She was looking directly into Rosa's eyes, and her expression was kind.

Rosa nodded. "Not too fast, but upbeat, yes."

The woman nodded. "Can you count it off?" When Rosa nodded, she smiled and said, "Just do your best. If we get it all wrong, they will let you start over once. Just stop and tell me what needs changing." Rosa curtsied again, grateful. Some audition pianists were bored and irritable.

Rosa went to center stage. She struck her pose, a stiff-legged stance of a tin soldier on watch duty. Arms behind her back, her posture ramrod straight. Once she was set, she lifted her right foot and used her tap to count off the beat.

Clickit, clickit, clickit, CLICK.

The pianist came in perfectly and precisely. Rosa turned in a stiff-legged circle, miming the movements of a wooden toy come to life. She saluted, her spine as straight as a ramrod, only her feet dancing the rhythm of the music, floating her over the polished wood floor.

Rosa elaborated the rhythm slightly as she turned front again, saluting sharply, then pivoting to stand with her back to the darkened expanse beyond the stage.

The pianist stayed on tempo exactly, but it was clear that she was watching Rosa, too, trying her best to amplify the dramatic parts of the routine. Rosa began to dance for her, to enjoy the duet between the pianist and her own two feet, the mix of melody and rhythm.

Rosa shuffled and tapped, her feet flying as the music carried her from one side of the stage to the other, then back to perfect center for a cartwheel and a picot, then a backbend that became a walkover, her taps clicking solidly as she came back onto her feet, her soldier's face stern and fixed, then breaking into a smile.

The smile was real. The dance Rosa had practiced a thousand times somehow felt new as she moved toward the centerpiece of her routine, a long sequence of steps that she had worked hard and long to master. She had taken bits of the Nicholas brothers' routines in *Flying Down to Rio*—and even though she'd had to change and simplify to be able to imitate the great dancers at all, she knew it looked good. She had made it her own, and was doing it as well as she could.

Sailing into the shim-sham that was the climax of her act, Rosa suddenly abandoned her stiff-legged soldier stance and styled low, her knees bent as she worked her way through the stomp-offs, pushes, Tack Annies, and half-breaks. She was lost in the music now, and in some little corner of her mind she knew she had never danced better at an audition. But that thought was distant, muted by the pure joy of the dance itself.

When the finish came, Rosa slid to the floor in perfect, flat-legged splits, then came up again and stiffened, resuming the stance of the toy soldier, her arm lifting in a single, precise salute.

The pianist finished, and there was only silence on the stage except for the sound of her own breathing. A few seconds later, she heard the sound of her mother talking in a low, urgent voice to the studio woman and the sound of her reply.

"Very good," a woman's voice came from below the stage, breaking the spell. Rosa peered forward. It was the woman star she couldn't recognize. No one had ever bothered to comment on her routine before. "You're too old for the lead, but there will be lots of dance numbers, some with solos from supporting players and other extras. Are you interested?"

"Oh, yes," Rosa breathed. Then she cleared her throat and said it more clearly.

"I'll look forward to seeing you on the set," the beautiful woman said, then pitched her voice at the matron. "Get her name and number from the mother." Then she waved her hand in dismissal. Rosa started back toward Mama, still breathing hard.

"Who is she?" Rosa whispered to the studio woman who was writing on her clipboard.

"Who?"

"The star," Rosa said. "The one who talked to me."

The studio woman laughed softly. "That's Frances Marion. She wrote the script and she's going to direct the film here if they can work the deal with MGM. If not, she'll do it over there, I expect."

Rosa glanced back. Miss Marion was talking to her companions now, laughing and chatting.

"The director?" Mama whispered. "She's the—"

"Yes," the studio woman said impatiently. "Now if you will let us continue?"

Rosa walked in a daze all the way home. Her mother was talking most of the way and she heard some of it, but it was hard to concentrate. She felt like someone had opened the sky and invited her inside. A woman director who wrote the scenarios, the very stories the movies were made from. She was really the one in charge of the scenes, the one who shaped the whole movie.

"You danced beautifully," Mama was saying over her shoulder. She was beaming, striding along. "Maybe you can get the lead in Miss Marion's next story if you shine on the set."

Rosa nodded because she didn't want to argue. But it wasn't leads she wanted now. She was beginning to know what her own dream was, and that made everything else fall into place. She had so much to learn. She wondered if there were books about how people made movies, about directing. And she wanted to write better and better stories. Were there books about writing screenplay scenarios? Miss Campbell would know. Mama would get used to the idea. She would just have to.

After a few blocks, Rosa ran a few steps to catch up and walk beside her mother. By the time they got to Hollywood Boulevard and were hurrying to catch the streetcar, she was leading the way.

Tuesday, June 26, 1934

This is the best, sunniest morning in a long time. Two good things have happened! Last night Pancho came by to say good-bye to me. It was sad, but also good to talk to him. He told me to forgive Mama for not telling me about Papa wanting a rancho and all the rest. He said her own dream is to be a star, but she is too afraid to even audition. So she wants me to do it for her.

I never thought about it like that, but it makes sense. That's why she gets so nervous at auditions. Pancho laughed and said he had heard of women directors, but that he had never worked with one— not on a Western movie. I told him he would have to come back from Mexico to work on my first Western production, and he said he would. He promised.

The second good thing is that the casting department called today, and I will have weeks of work as a chorus dancer and as an extra on Miss Marion's movie. I can't wait. I am going to learn everything I can from watching her.

Last night I told Mama I want to be a director, and she just smiled and said being the star is better. But I want to make movies, not just star in them.

Mama, if you read this, I love you, but if you want to be a star, you have to audition. Pancho says I can love you very much and still follow my own heart. I hope he's right.

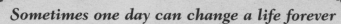

Sometimes one day can change a life forever

American Diaries

**Different girls,
living in different periods of America's past
reveal their hearts' secrets in the pages
of their diaries. Each one faces a challenge
that will change her life forever.
Don't miss any of their stories:**

SURVIVAL

Would you get out alive?

FACED WITH DISASTER, ORDINARY PEOPLE FIND UNTAPPED DEPTHS OF COURAGE AND DETERMINATION THEY NEVER DREAMED THEY POSSESSED.

Find Adventure in these books!

#1 TITANIC

On a clear April night hundreds of passengers on the *Titanic* find themselves at the mercy of a cold sea. Few will live to remember the disaster—will Gavin and Karolina be among the survivors?

#2 EARTHQUAKE

Can two strangers from very different worlds work together to survive the terror of the quake—crumbling buildings, fire, looting, and chaos?

#3 BLIZZARD

Can a Rocky Mountain rancher's daughter and her rich, spoiled cousin stop arguing long enough to cooperate to survive a sudden, vicious blizzard?

#4 FIRE

Fate and fire throw Nate and Julie together on the dark streets of Chicago. Now they must find a way out before the flames spreading across the city cut off their only chance of escape!

ALSO:

#5 FLOOD
#6 DEATH VALLEY
#7 CAVE-IN

#8 TRAIN WRECK
#9 HURRICANE
#10 FOREST FIRE

#11 SWAMP

Simon & Schuster Children's Publishing Division
where imaginations meet
www.SimonSaysKids.com

American Diaries